ICELAND

ICELAND

Dominic Hoey

STEELE ROBERTS
A O T E A R O A

ISBN 978-0-947493-43-1
A catalogue record for this book is available from the
National Library of New Zealand.

Cover designed by Roy Irwin.
Author photo: Paul Taylor.
Text layout and design by Sarah Bolland.
Printed in Wellington by PrintStop.

STEELE ROBERTS AOTEAROA
Box 9321 Wellington, Aotearoa New Zealand
info@SteeleRoberts.co.nz • www.SteeleRoberts.co.nz

to Kristina

68 ZLATA

THIS ALL HAPPENED five or six years ago. I was at some party, another in an endless celebration of life. The decaying villa stank of sex and cigarettes. I had my guitar with me, determined to make the most of that Sunday before dragging myself back to my awful job. I was playing covers of songs for beers, making up half the chords and lyrics, drunk and excited. People fell in and out of the cluttered living room all night, screaming in tongues, laughing as the small house shook. It was one of those parties where different pockets of Auckland came together and if you drank enough and squinted real hard, you could pretend you were part of a real city.

I had just finished a terrible version of 'Pink Frost', and when I looked up you were standing in front of me in an old black T-shirt and paint-stained jeans, your long limbs dirty with faded tattoos. I'd seen you checking me out all night from across the room, where you stood huddled with a group of dodgy-looking guys and a small, loud girl. As the night began to lose focus, I gave up hope that I'd get to talk you and then there you were.

"I'm Hamish."

"Zlata." I was tuning my guitar.

"Zlata …" you repeated, running your tongue over the curves of the letters. "That's an out-of-it name."

"My mother wasn't born here." I strummed a G chord. "Do you want to hear a song?"

"Sure."

"Which one? I know them all."

"'Waiting Round to Die.'"

"I actually do know that one," I said, surprised by your request. And so I played amongst the madness of that night.

* * *

"Do you wanna go for a swim?" you asked when I finished. I could see your friends watching from across the room.

I clutched my guitar to my chest and smiled. I noticed then you had the saddest eyes.

"There's this pool … it's behind some office blocks on College Hill."

I didn't tell you I was afraid of drowning.

"It'll be fun."

The night was warm. We drank and talked of nothing, my guitar over my shoulder. I let you lead me down streets I'd known all my life, hoping it wouldn't be another dead end. When we arrived at the pool it was a dirty green, filled with rotting flowers and leaves. It didn't seem to bother you and I felt stupid for caring. I was watching you take off your T-shirt when we were chased away by a fat security guard. We ran from the minimum-wage authority figure, laughing and holding hands. I wish I could say we got away, but that would be lying.

We spent most of that night in a skate park drinking a bottle of expensive whisky you had materialised out of nowhere. I remember thinking I should go home. I'd been late for work all the previous week. But it would have been easier to walk up to the moon that had been following us than to leave your side. You had an easy laugh that interrupted the stories of your life you told me. They were all wild, filled with violence and chaos. Even though I hated fighting and all that stupidity, I found myself fascinated when you described your adventures. I talked about my music. The album I was working on, my one-woman band called Picnic, my dreams of getting a record deal. You listened so attentively. And then I kissed you in that concrete bowl while the moon watched on.

* * *

We woke up naked in my bed.

"Where are we?" you asked.

"I don't know," I replied, hugging you tightly, feeling weightless when you squeezed me back.

I called in sick and we drank all afternoon in Grey Lynn Park. I talked so fast I kept stumbling, scared to leave space for my anxieties. Your phone rang over and over but you ignored it.

"Aren't you going to answer?" I asked the fifth time it rang.

"Nah, it's not important," you said, pushing the phone away.

You were quieter in the daylight, giving little away, except when you kissed me. Your touch was gentle, in contrast to the bluntness of your words. You were complete in a way most men I knew back then weren't. You couldn't be anyone but yourself. At the time that seemed like the most exciting thing in the world.

* * *

By dusk I was drunk. As the streetlights woke up, we wandered the neighbourhood we'd both grown up in. Everything was painted new in your presence, gone the dull familiarity that normally coated Grey Lynn. My stomach was filled with alcohol and excitement, and despite the fact I was wearing the same jeans and T-shirt as last night, I felt fresh. Growing up, you had lived across the park from me and we tried to work out if we'd met before. Walking down Williamson Ave, holding hands, I craned my neck every few minutes to look into those sad eyes. You smiled whenever you caught me, giving my hand a squeeze. We stopped at a flat I used to live in when I still counted on tomorrow. The solid white house looked the same but when I ran my hand over the weatherboards the wood came away like wet paper.

"Look," I said, holding my hand up. You furrowed your brow in confusion.

"Look at what?"

"My hand."

You shrugged your shoulders.

"Let's climb on my roof and watch the sunset," I said, changing the subject.

How quickly our past becomes a metaphor for the present.

67 HAMISH

FUCK, I'M HUNGOVER. I don't wanna lift my head off the pillow. I run my paint-stained fingers through Zlata's thick, dark hair. She's on the phone to someone. Rapley keeps texting. He's pissed off. We were supposed to be getting paint for this new wall he's found. I don't feel like going anywhere. Zlata's room is filled with books. There's a giant photo of her and a couple of other girls standing on top of a hill in the rain. They're laughing. I think I recognise one of them.

"Yes, I know. Look, I'll be there tomorrow. What? Okay. *Okay*, I said." Zlata throws the phone on the floor, rolls onto her back.

"Jesus!" she says, "You'd think I worked for fucking NASA or something, the way they go on."

"What's your job?"

"Working at this office. The most boring, pointless job in the actual world." We kiss. "What do you do for work?" Zlata looks at me, her big eyes so blue on her round face.

"You know, this and that." I sit up and roll a joint of this new shit Rapley's been getting.

"How vague and mysterious. Can you give me a clue?"

"I'll tell you some other time."

"So we're going to hang out more?"

"If you wanna." I light the joint and lie back.

"Nah, you suck. I don't want to see you again."

"Whatever ..."

"I'm joking."

"I know."

"But you should tell me what your job is. I have to have something to tell my friends other than you're hot and a weedhead."

"What? Nah, this is just for my hangover."

"Yeah, yeah. Do you mind if I sleep some more?"

"Nah, sweet."

She smiles. "I like the way you talk."

I don't know what she means, but it makes me feel good.

66 ZLATA

"SO DID YOU fuck him?" Hayley screamed in my ear. We were standing in the middle of the dance floor of some shitty club that'd appeared out of nowhere a few months back. A lone disco ball hung in place above us.

Hayley had bought an expensive bottle of champagne. We passed it back and forth while moving lazily to the music, my feet sticking to the floor with each step.

"Maybe," I smiled.

"Good for you," she said, "I hate seeing you miserable."

I took the bottle off her, ignoring the barbed compliment. Someone bumped into me, spilling beer down my jeans.

Hayley and I had come from a ridiculous restaurant downtown that neither of us could afford. She spent most of the dinner staring into her phone, relaying bits of gossip to me. All around us rich people in suits and expensive dresses howled with laughter, ripping flesh from dead animals with their fingers. It was the first night we'd spent apart since we met a week before. You'd gone off on a secret mission that afternoon, muttering about shit to do when I questioned you. I was trying to not let my imagination run off with my good mood, so I distracted myself by listening to Hayley rant on about the personal lives of people I didn't know.

The DJ played a rap song that was popular at the time and the whole club started jumping up and down. I suddenly felt exhausted.

"I'm off," I said, handing the bottle back to Hayley.

"Use a condom!" she yelled after me.

* * *

It felt like the city was under curfew, the streets empty apart from the rubbish that danced in circles above cigarette butts and broken bottles. A taxi drove past, slowing to stare at me. I remember feeling like I was floating that night, as though I too could be lifted and spun around with the chip packets and yesterday's news.

I'd been feeling down so long it was novel to smile. This was different than the drugged happiness my doctor kept prescribing with an intense concern.

* * *

My flat smelt like damp wood and perfume.

I put on track pants and grabbed my guitar. I'd been trying to finish my album for months. The five songs I had were okay, you said you liked them. But people wouldn't want to hear an entire album about my dead-end job and boring ex.

Labels weren't exactly lining up to sign me, but every show people would ask to buy my music, so it seemed like I should try to make something.

I sat down on the edge of my unmade bed and started working on a new idea. At first it was just random words and chords moving in and out of each other. Then things started to come together. The words became sentences, became verses and eventually a song. I was almost finished when I realised it was about you, us, those first few nights.

65 HAMISH

RAPLEY'S WALKING ROUND the paint store looking sketchy. I fill my bag with cans. He's so tall I can see his cap over the top of the shelves. Two of the workers are following him, leaving only one for me to avoid. I'm wearing my best preppy outfit, but the shitty tattoos on my hands will give me away if they look hard enough. My bag's full. I'm trying to leave without the cans making that rattling noise. I start to relax as I step into the afternoon sun. Ducking down Ariki Street I take off my white dress shirt and stuff it in the bag with the cans. A few minutes later, Rapley wanders round the corner.

"Man those losers were persistent," he says, leaning against the wall.

"All good, got heaps bro."

"Sweet …" I throw the backpack over my shoulder and we head down towards his place.

Rapley's my oldest friend. He grew up one house up from me; a falling-down green villa full of noise and extended family. When I was little I probably spent more time there than at my own place. My house was dead. My father fucked off overseas, my mother lost to booze and bitterness. Rapley still lives in that same house with his older brother and two cousins. His auntie moved south a few years back, rented the house to them. His place had a sweet, rotting fragrance. A lot of houses I went to as a child smelt the same. I got no idea what it was. Now it stinks of weed, feet and cheap deodorant. I dump my backpack on his bed.

"Why did you get so much pink?" Rapley says, picking up the cans and tossing them back on the bed.

"It looks red on the can."

"Are you colour blind? That shit is obviously pink."

"Shut up, it's all good."

"Maybe for your shitty style."

"Whatever."

Rapley sits down on the bed, making the cans rattle. He grabs a big bag of buds off his desk and starts rolling a joint.

"Did you hook up with that girl from the party?" Me and Rapley talk about everything, but I feel shy all of a sudden. "The one playing the guitar. She had a nice voice."

"Yeah." My voice comes out all weird. "She's really cool."

"Nice." Rapley sparks the joint. "She have any friends?" he says, laughing.

"Shut up." I smile.

"We should hit up that wall I was telling you about."

He passes me the joint.

"Where is it?"

"Just behind the supermarket. It's a good spot."

I've always loved graffiti. Something comforting about seeing the names of people you love and hate when you're out. Makes a city feel lived in.

Me and Rapley spent our childhood up on Surrey Crescent, playing spacies, eating fish and chips, walking for hours round the streets, shoplifting, doing shitty tags, talking 'bout what would happen when we grew up. In a fucked-up way, we've become what we wanted to be; artists who answer to no one, 'cept maybe WINZ.

64 ZLATA

WE SPENT THOSE first weeks in my bed with the tiny heater struggling to fight back the chill. I'd leave for the office in the morning while you lay there protesting and grabbing at me, half asleep. All day I'd sit at my desk pretending to work, thinking of you till five when I would all but run to the bus stop.

Sometimes I'd get home to find you still in bed, drawing and smoking weed. Other nights you'd have a bottle of wine and pizza waiting, and some adventure planned.

In those early weeks, we'd often get high and take walks at night. You, distracted and present at the same time, while I talked endlessly of music and travel. The city felt different when I explored it with you. There were streets that would only appear when I was in your company. Walls that during the daytime would sink back into the ground, shortcuts that would dry up beneath the sun. You were on good terms with the night and it felt welcoming in your presence.

"You remember when that was a spacies parlour?" You gestured at a Pizza Hutt on Surrey Crescent.

"A what?"

"Spacies."

"You mean like video games?"

"Yeah."

"No. We had a computer when I was young."

"Flash."

We walked up towards the library. A group of shadows watched from the other side of the street. I felt myself tense. You noticed and looked over at them.

"Don't worry about those fucking toys," you hissed, spreading your shoulders, your voice dropping. We passed them and you returned to your normal tone. "Man, me and Rapley used to spend all our money back there. Street Fighter, Mortal Kombat, clocked all of those games."

"Nerd."

"What?"

I laughed at the hurt in your voice. "You were just a poor computer nerd."

"Nah, fucking …" You stopped yourself, realising you were being teased. "You're funny," you said, hugging me.

"So are you, dingbat."

We stopped in front of some graffiti that said 'Ray' on the side of a wall on Great North.

"That's Rapley's," you said, proudly.

"I want to meet your friends."

"I don't know if you'll like them."

"It doesn't matter."

"Nah, I guess not."

* * *

I loved that your anxieties were only for the moment, as though you had no concept of tomorrow. I guess in the end, this, coupled with my constant need for change, led to the current situation. But at the time it was new and different.

My last serious boyfriend, Charlie, lived in his head. He was an academic, even wore a suit jacket with jeans. His speciality was some kind of obscure postmodern philosophy that made me want to poke my eyes out whenever he talked about it. Everything was picked clean, leaving the bare bones for me to survive on. Every conversation and action had to be deconstructed to the point that I wanted to kill him. That was when the drinking started, I guess. Or maybe it was earlier. Either way, things with Charlie descended into a convenient hell. I would go into the office during daylight and stare at the monitor, so numb you could have cut me and I wouldn't have flinched. In the dark I'd drink in front of the TV, trading one screen for another, until I passed out. My mother was shocked by my sunken eyes and despondent attitude. She paid for me to go see a shrink, a small authoritative woman who talked in clichés and put me on antidepressants. By some miracle I still wrote occasionally during this time, and it was the songs that convinced me to leave.

I remember listening to my demos one night, pissed on red wine. The songs were all about death and escape. The next morning when Charlie was at work I packed up what little I owned and moved in with my brother. I didn't even leave a note. My revenge for him driving me insane was cruelty. Over the coming months I broke him in two, laughing when he tried to intellectualise my leaving. I can't believe I once thought I loved him. In hindsight, does anyone's life not look like a series of stupid mistakes?

* * *

"What's postmodern mean?" you asked one night in bed.

"Why do you ask?"

"It says it on that book," you said, pointing at one of Charlie's textbooks I had been meaning to throw out.

"It's hard to explain."

"You don't even know," you laughed.

"It's like something that's self-aware."

"Say what?"

"Well, okay … so, like, there's no absolute truth, right. If you reduce things to opposites, one will always be greater than the other."

"I'm confused."

"It's not worth worrying about. I like how you don't care about that carry-on. It's refreshing."

"'Bout what?"

"Just intellectual nonsense."

"I'm jealous of your brain."

"Whatever."

"It's true. I like that you're so brainy." You kissed me and gently ran your hand over my stomach.

I wanted to protest. Tell you that I went to Suicide High, where the motto was 'Fly or Burn — producing Auckland's mad women and men since 1977'. And then university for a few years where I drank and danced my way to a B-minus average. But you seemed so proud of my imagined intelligence and by the time I'd thought about all of this, you were inside me.

63 HAMISH

"YO, BABY," JAMIL SAYS in his annoying nasal voice. I'm cutting through the park on the way to the studio. Jamil's on his bench with Skam, an opened box of beers next to him. I was trying to sneak past. He's a small fat bastard, without sense or sanity. His chubby face looks innocent, like an angel, but he's a fucking psycho. I walk over slowly. Skam runs his fingers over his wispy moustache. He wears a mix of brand-new stolen clothes and paint-stained hand-me-downs that hang off his skinny frame. Looks like he got dressed in the dark.

"Hey, guys."

"My man," says Jamil in a tone that's both serious and taking the piss. I get trapped in some stupid handshake involving clicking. Skam raises his eyebrows in acknowledgment.

"What's happening?" I ask.

"Just drinking some very best and watching a quality sports event," Jamil says, pointing with one of his fat pink hands to the field. A bunch of guys are running unco-ordinatedly after a soccer ball.

"One of them's in the All Whites," he adds.

"Bullshit."

"Yeah, nah, it's true," Jamil's voice gets even more high-pitched. "The ginger, he was in the World Cup."

"Want a beer?" Skam asks.

"Nah, I'm on a mission."

"What, you after some buds?"

"Nah bro."

On the field someone gets the ball, freaks out and kicks it onto the road.

"You doing much painting?" Skam asks.

I have, but it's of Zlata. Fuck talking 'bout my love life with these two idiots. Anyway, that's not the kind of painting he means.

"Not heaps."

"FUCK! THERE HE GOES!" Jamil yells, jumping out of his seat, spilling beer on my T-shirt. "RUN, YA FUCKING GINGE CUNT!" he screams. The redhead's got the ball, sprinting towards two piles of clothing that act as goalposts. He turns, looks at us, running straight into one of the other players.

"Fuck, he's a disgrace," Skam mutters, looking away in disgust.

"I got to bounce."

We slap hands again and I leave.

* * *

Rapley's up in our tiny studio on K Road, a wooden box filled with beer bottles, paint and weirdos. One of them,

Luke, is there when I arrive. He's a skinny 17-year-old with frizzy blond hair who's always hanging around. He bought some weed off me a couple of years back and somehow we ended up adopting him. He's cool, more on to it than most of the kids who hang around up here.

The place stinks. There's paintings all over the walls, and a huge work table covered in tags and rubbish takes up the centre of the room. Opposite the door, filthy windows look out onto Myers Park. Rapley's working on a big canvas with a clown vomiting money. A shitty computer almost as old as Luke sits in one corner playing country music.

"'Sup." I chuck my bag on the desk.

"Hey man," Rapley says, not looking up.

"Hey ya bastard," Luke squawks.

I give him a hug. "You should be at school — don't wanna end up being an artist."

"I got kicked out again."

"For what?"

"Smoking weed."

"Why you getting high at school? You'd have gone to the park, dick." I put on Hank Williams.

"Like you would've," Luke says, getting defensive.

"It's not the point. I'm imparting some wisdoms here."

"It'd be a sad day when anyone listens to your bullshit advice," Rapley snorts.

I get out my paints and start working on the portrait of Zlata.

"Who's the babe?" Luke asks.

"My girlfriend."

"Is she that hot in real life?"

"Hotter."

"Awww," they both say.

"You're in love," Luke says, picking up his guitar, strumming, yelling, "LOVE, LOVE, LOVE, LOVE."

"Fuck up, dick." I throw a spray can at him, hitting his guitar.

"Be careful, this was a lovely birthday present."

"Zlata wants to meet you," I tell Rapley.

"What about me?" Luke asks.

"No one's trying to meet you, fucknuts," Rapley says, still working on his painting.

"Her mate's having a party tomorrow. We should go."

"Maybe."

"Can I come?" whines Luke.

"Only if you get Rapley to come."

Luke starts strumming his guitar again. "Come to the party, come to the party, come to the party."

* * *

It must be past midnight. Me and Rapley are still up at the studio, sitting at the window, looking out onto the street. Some woman's screaming at her boyfriend. We share a joint, watching their domestic.

"Hey, before I forget, there's a show in a few months. Wanted to see if you're down. Me and you," he says, putting one of his massive hands on my shoulder.

"I don't know."

"Come on, man, your new work's really good."

"Thanks, but I haven't got many pieces."

"So, you don't have a job, you got plenty of time."

"Let me think about it."

"Sweet. But you got to do it."

I go over to the work table and start measuring out

coke. Rapley's still at the window, texting some girl. His love life's complicated.

"Bro, she reckons come over after one."

"It's almost 12 now."

"I guess." I finish up the last bag, put them in a metal tin, stuff the tin into an old sneaker and toss it on top of the shelf.

"The cops will never find that," Rapley says.

"I'll just tell them you sold it to me."

"When you gonna find another way to make money?"

"I don't know," I say, doing a bump off the table.

Rapley's phone beeps.

"Now she's saying two. Fuck that. I'm gonna hit up Leah."

"The one with the babies?"

"Yeah. Check this out." He holds up his phone; a blurry picture of someone's breasts fills the screen.

"Tits," I say.

"Yes, Hamish. She's hot, right?"

"Sure." I put the scales back in the cupboard.

"Okay, I'm out, man."

"You going to come tomorrow?"

Rapley stops by the door. "Only 'cos I love you and I'm not staying all night."

"I'm sure they'll kick us out before then," I say.

He laughs, hugging me.

"Take care, brother." The phone beeps again. "Man, she's not even home," he cries as he walks out the door.

* * *

I never planned on doing this for a living. Didn't plan to do anything really. We left school, went on the dole and did graff 24/7. Because we were getting better, making a name, it felt like we were achieving something. It wasn't until I started looking for a job that I realised the trap I'd fallen into. So when the chance to start selling came up, it wasn't really much of a choice. At first it was just weed. But the mark-up's so small, it's impossible to make any real money. I got Rapley to introduce me to his cousins, who are patched up. He made me promise it was just short-term till I sussed out something else. That was four years ago.

62 ZLATA

THE NIGHT OF Hayley's party, the city was on fire. I watched it burn from the bay windows in the lounge. In the bedroom I changed into my green dress. Staring into the mirror, I felt alive for the first time in years.

Hayley's house was beautiful. Her parents bought it for next to nothing in the '80s. When too many other rich people moved into the neighbourhood they fled west to Titirangi, leaving the house to Hayley and her two sisters: Christina, who was reported to have a drug problem, as if that was something unusual; and Alice, who had two children and a borderline perverse lust for life. The house was two-storeyed and hung out over the footpath in a precarious manner, emulating the lifestyles of its inhabitants. The top storey was surrounded by a rickety verandah, where many nights were spent drinking and talking about sex and the future. The interior was all polished wood and antique fittings. It was the kind of place you usually got kicked out of for spilling wine on the sofa.

When I arrived, Alice was sitting at the kitchen table pouring spirits into an orange plastic bowl. She wore a shiny silver dress that hugged her voluptuous frame with all its might.

"Hey, honey," she called out as I shuffled in, "you look great tonight."

"Thanks, so do you." I took a seat at the kitchen table.

"So Hayley tells me you have a new beau." Alice adjusted her dress. It looked like it had once belonged to someone who knew how to dance.

"Yeah, Hamish. He might come tonight," I said, distracted by her impressive cleavage.

"Exciting." She emptied the last bottle into the bowl.

"Where are the little ones?"

"With their dad, so there's going to be nonstop fun."

"Awesome."

"Why didn't you bring your guitar?"

"Shit, I didn't even think."

Hayley walked into the room. Her long black dress was cut low in the front and back, her hair curled, her eyes heavy with make-up.

"Whoa!" Alice cried.

"Way to upstage everyone, bitch."

"What, this old thing?" Hayley said. "Come here, stranger." I got up and hugged her.

"I never see you any more."

"I know, I've been useless."

"So is he coming?"

"I think so. He said he might bring some of his pals."

"That's cool. He's an artist, right?" She took a seat at the table with rehearsed grace.

"Yeah, I mean he does graffiti." Hayley's face fell like a badly hung painting.

"Don't be judgmental."

"As long as he doesn't tag the house," she said, smiling again. "So, what else?"

"About Hamish? Ummm, I don't know. He's really sweet, handsome. He's inspiring in a crazy way."

"Jealous," Alice said, pouring punch with a ladle.

"So what about you?" I asked, taking a sip of the sweet, red liquid.

"Nothing exciting. Working, been on some dates, but you know."

"Where's Christina?"

"Upstairs. God I hope she's not a dick tonight. Did you hear about the shoplifting thing?"

"Yeah."

"She's lucky we have this place or she'd probably be on the street."

"That's a bit much," Alice said.

"Stop defending her all the time."

"I'm not, but you always paint her in such a bad light and I think …"

"Okay, okay, let's get drunk," I said, defusing the situation.

* * *

You staggered in around eleven. I saw you swaying in the doorway. A large Polynesian guy, handsome with a tough, regal air, stood behind you, looking vaguely uncomfortable. Peering over his broad shoulders was a tall, skinny kid with wild blond hair and an acoustic guitar.

"Baby," you said, spotting me from across the room. You had never called me that before and it made my stomach warm. You ambled through the room full of art students dancing badly to hip hop with your strange walk; half limp, half strut, and kissed me. You tasted sweet.

"This is my boy, Rapley."

Rapley put out his hand, but I ignored it and hugged him. "Oh … okay," he chuckled, hugging me back.

"And this fool's Luke."

"Hello," the kid said shyly, staying well back. Everyone at the party had stopped dancing and was staring, and I suddenly felt bad for inviting you. But you were too drunk to notice.

"What have you been doing?"

"Just out doing … stuff," you said, swaying side to side. Rapley and the kid stood back, aware of the eyes crawling over them. I saw Hayley leaning against the wall by the stereo, watching us with a smirk. I waved her over.

"Hayley, this is Hamish."

"Hello," she said, pecking you on the cheek.

"And this is Rapley and … sorry, I forgot your name."

"Just call him dickhead," you said, pulling a full bottle of whisky out from the front of your pants.

"So, you're an artist?" Hayley said.

"Nah, he's the artist," you pointed at Rapley before opening the bottle, taking a swig and screwing up your face. "I just tag shit."

Rapley smiled uneasily.

"Oh, okay, well, welcome," Hayley turned and walked back towards the stereo.

"That went well," I said, taking the bottle off you and gulping down a mouthful.

61 HAMISH

ME AND RAPLEY are siting in a shitty bar smashing one beer after another. The nerdy-looking bartender is playing some '80s pop record that keeps skipping. Apart from us, the place is empty. Rapley's teasing me and trying to find someone to fuck.

"What were you thinking?" he says, "Punching that poor dude like that. He was smaller than Luke."

"I know."

"Was a good hit though."

"Yeah."

"He really flew."

"He asked if we were homies."

"Homos?"

"Nah, homies. Like thugs."

"Who the fuck still says homies."

"I don't know, I was drunk."

"Yes, you were."

"She won't text me back."

"No wonder, man. You fucked up the whole party. Those girls were crying, old 'are you a homie' got blood everywhere, fucking Luke puked in the kitchen."

"I was nervous." I finish my beer, order two more. Rapley gets a text.

"Yeah, it's on."

"With who?"

"Kate."

"Which one's she?"

"The hot one, thing's sister's friend."

"Who, Sarah?"

"Nah — the one with the tattoos."

"I got no idea who you're talking about." A group of young girls stumble in, squealing. They spot me and Rapley staring at them. One waves, they all burst out laughing, fall into a booth. My phone rings.

"It's Jamil."

"'Sup."

"You holding?"

"Yeah."

"Meet at yours in 30?"

"Cool."

"Yeah, bitches." The phone goes dead.

"I'm off." I scull my beer. "Bills to pay."

"You should quit that shit, bro." Rapley shakes his head.

"I know, I know."

"Let's do this exhibition and make some money," he calls as I leave.

As I walk out I see him slip into the booth with the girls.

* * *

I'm paying double the rent I was five years ago. I share a
two-bedroom house with an angry gang of rats and Bella,
a small girl with messy red hair and an animated face. She's
a photographer, wasting her days in a shoe store. Her walls
are covered in snapshots of her life. We're all there: Rapley
when he went through his cornrows phase; me with jeans
so big you could fit one person in each leg.

Me and Bella have been friends since meeting in
remedial maths at school. We used to sneak out and smoke
weed in Western Springs Park with the other future dole
bludgers and minimum-wage losers.

Sitting by the lake, we'd talk about our dreams.

Everyone was going to be a famous musician or artist.

They probably should have had classes on realistic
expectations. But some people came close, made a little
money.

These days, the only one from remedial maths who still
dreams is Rapley.

* * *

Bella's in the kitchen eating pasta with her girlfriend, Jean
— she's tall and sporty with chronic verbal diarrhoea and
an endless supply of tracksuits. She plays some kind of
sport semi-professionally, I forget which one.

"Hello," they both chime when I walk in.

"Hey." I open the fridge and get a beer.

"What's going on?" Bella asks. "You look down."

"Think I fucked things up with Zlata."

"Already? That was quick."

"I know. Punched her mate."

"That'll do it," she laughs.

"You should take her something," Jean says. "A nice present."

"Yeah, and take her to dinner, go to that Thai place."

"Which one?"

"The nice one."

"With the yummy spring rolls," says Jean.

"Up the road?"

"Yeah, take her there and get her drunk. Maybe you could not wear a hat and brush your hair?"

I open my beer and sit down.

"I've made her a painting. Maybe I could give her that."

"Perfect," says Bella, "and then take her to dinner."

* * *

"You met the American yet?" Jamil asks. He's sitting on my bed, his feet dangling off the edge.

"Nah, man."

"Yeah, he's a real American. You know how they dress, smart casual, and talks like he's off the TV." He's got a small bat he brought with him, flipping it over, catching it by the handle. His tiny blue shorts cling to the tops of his fat white thighs.

"He was at the bar the other night," he continues. "Think he knows old Sam."

"Sam girl or Sam boy?"

"The slut."

"Don't call her that; she's my friend."

"So, she's still a slut."

"Whatever." I hand him the plastic bag of pills and take his money.

"You see those DMT faggots capped your piece?"

"Which one?"

"By the supermarket. Rapley's going to be pissed."

DMT … I can't even remember what that shit stands for, so many three-letter acronyms. Some rich kids trying to be tough.

"We'll catch up with them," I say, counting the cash.

"I heard you're in love," Jamil says, an evil grin on his fat face.

"I don't know."

"And that there was a scrap at some rich girl's house."

"I don't want to talk about it."

"You steal some shit?"

"Nah, wasn't like that."

"When there's a fight is the best time to rack shit. Everyone's like it's not worth it, calm down. In the commotion you just take what you want."

"Where's Skam?" I change the subject.

"Out west with his folks," Jamil says bitterly.

Skam's tight with his family. It's a sore point with Jamil. He's banned from his and Skam's family homes for being a little psycho. Actually, Jamil's pretty much banned from everywhere. Skam's real name's Sonny. No one calls him that. His parents live in Mangere with his two younger brothers, Te Waa and Manu. Both parents are youth workers, trying to stop the local fuck-ups from going to jail. Waa does carvings while Manu teaches at a primary school. Everyone likes to guess the poison secret that made Skam a mute lunatic, but no one really knows.

"You going to the party on the weekend?" asks Jamil.

"Whose is it?"

"I don't know, it's in Mt Eden somewhere."

"Maybe."

"Maybe," he copies me. "Maybe, maybe, maybe," he repeats, strutting out the door, whacking the wall with his bat.

I fall on the bed, exhausted and heartbroken.

60 ZLATA

NOBODY EVER REALLY LEAVES. Sure some people get out but you still see them wandering the streets; former lovers, flatmates, friends, enemies. I talk to them sometimes, have that same argument once more for luck, or apologise for some drunken indiscretion that happened twelve years earlier. Even those that stay and grow old here are revisited by their youthful selves. There's nothing like walking down Sussex Street on a drunken Thursday night and bumping into the 21-year-old you to cause a minor crisis. In my mind's eye, I'm always just a less wrinkled, skinnier version of my current self, but suddenly there I am, dancing down the street towards me, laughing and weightless, almost unrecognisable. I think of how my worries back then were about the most inconsequential things, blissfully unaware of how bad it was going to get. When I see this combination of inexperience and ignorance face to face, I can't help falling in love with the simplicity of a life that never existed, seduced by nostalgia's fragmented beauty. This is the price of living in a graveyard.

To say Hayley's party was a disaster is an under-statement. I didn't really care about the fight. Jacob, who you punched, was a spoilt sex-pest. You were so drunk and everyone was being so rude, something was bound to happen. Jacob's nose was broken, but so what? It gave him a bit of character.

Just before the fight, Christina came downstairs looking every bit the mad woman she is, dressed in a tiny black mini-skirt, a white singlet and a man's camo jacket to top it all off. Her hair was tied in a topknot and her eyes looked like they were struggling to stay in their sockets. She stopped when she reached the bottom of the stairs.

"Hamish!" she yelled when she spotted you. You recoiled from her and glanced back at me.

"Do you guys know each other?" I asked.

"Nah, what?"

I looked at Christina, who was staring at you with a what-the-fuck look on her face. I turned back and caught you shaking your head.

"What's going on?"

"What?" you spluttered.

Then the weird kid threw up all over the floor in the kitchen.

* * *

I woke up the next morning to a fistful of apologies on my phone, each one more frantic than the last. I took my happy pills, showered and thought about the pros and cons of forgiving you. I didn't want another man in my life who stole my time and affection. But then again, you were so kind and exciting. I made toast and listened to National Radio. Outside it rained, as it always did. My head hurt. I started working on a new song, trying to ignore the phone. But every time it beeped I had to check it. Your messages were so sweet, all earnest and misspelt. I turned one of your texts into lyrics and worked on the song till Hayley turned up in the afternoon.

* * *

"You just have shit taste in men." In my tiny lounge we ate rich chocolate cake Hayley had bought from some expensive bakery.

"That's not very nice." The melody I'd just written still danced through my head, distracting me.

"But it's true."

I looked up at Hayley. Her disguise was perfect. Everything about her screamed money: the designer-label black jeans, the little handbag that cost more than everything I owned, the perfume from France that made you feel a little drunk if you got too close. She had wanted to act once, but slowly that dream was lost to drunken nights and small compromises. She always tried to push me in the same direction too, telling me I should take the job at the office as I was almost 30 and couldn't just waste my life on music. I'm ashamed to say I relented. I'd just broken up with Charlie and was feeling lost. Then she introduced me to the sadist, a sharp-featured man whose only qualities were money and cruelty. She spun fairytales of how handsome and smart he was. And when I spoke of his dull meanness she would roll her eyes, saying that's how men are. Then I met you.

But I shouldn't paint her as a bad person. She was a good friend in her way. When I really lost it she had sat with me for hours doing her nails and telling me to stop crying. She had loaned me money, fed me, driven me to gigs.

"The cake's nice."

"What? Don't change the subject."

"What do you want me to say?" I ask. "It's shit, but these things happen."

"I'm just worried about you."

"I'm fine."

She sighed loudly and looked around the room. "Okay. I got work tonight so I'm going to go rest," she said, getting to her feet. I walked her to the door and watched her strut up the road.

59 HAMISH

I FUCKING HATE WINZ. The dude in front of me smells like piss. Everyone's staring at the ground or checking their cheap phones. The line hasn't moved in fucking ages. Up front a trans woman is arguing with the bored case worker.

"My money was supposed to be in yesterday!" she's yelling, inches away from his pock-marked face.

"Your benefit has been suspended because you missed your meeting."

"But I made the appointment."

"And you didn't turn up to it."

"Because I was busy, I called up."

"I'm sorry." The two eyeball each other. I hope she punches him, but she spins on her heels and storms out.

"Next."

The man who smells like piss steps up. Rapley always says I don't need the sickness benefit. I make okay money. But I figure it's good for tax purposes, show some sort of income.

"Next."

"My name's Hamish Clulee, I have an appointment."

"Okay, take a seat."

I grab a pamphlet about joining the army. One of the boys signed up a few years ago. They kicked him out when they found he had a criminal record. It seems like the perfect job for criminals to me.

"Hamish." My case manager, Guy, is standing in front of me.

"Hey, bro."

"Hello." He is tall and nervous. Where do they find these people?

"Thinking of joining the army?" He looks at the pamphlet.

"Nah, bro, I'm a pacifist."

We sit at his desk. He's typing with one finger. Guy always has trouble with the computers. He finally gets my file up.

"Okay, Hamish, so you've been on the sickness benefit for four years?"

"Yep."

"And before that you were on the unemployment benefit for six years?"

"I think so."

"And before that the youth benefit for another couple of years?"

"True."

"At the moment we're really trying to get people off income support and back into the workforce."

"Yeah, but I got depression."

"What does your doctor say?"

"He says it's bad."

"Well, we'd like to send you to one of our doctors."

"Really?"

"There's an appointment available today."

"Yeah, whatever."

"I'm just trying to help you."

"I don't think this is helping my depression, Guy."

"Work is good for you."

* * *

The WINZ doctor's a middle-aged woman with cracked lips. Her office is white, with medical diagrams and a watercolour of a tree on the walls.

"So, how long have you been depressed?"

"Ages."

"Can you give me a number?"

"Since I left home, I guess."

"When was that?"

"Sixteen."

"Why did you leave home so young?"

"It was depressing."

She writes something on her computer and looks back up at me. "Do you take the medication Doctor ..." she looks at my file, "... Carson has been prescribing?"

"Yeah."

"And you don't drink with it? Because if you drink it won't work."

"Nah, no drinking."

I can tell she doesn't believe me. "So, what your case manager wants is to get you back into the workforce."

"There's no jobs."

"That's not true."

"My friend Bella has a degree and she sells shoes."

"Nevertheless, you can't stay on the benefit your whole life."

"But I'm depressed."

"I don't think sitting around at home all day is going to help. I'm going to sign you up for one more month."

"Don't fucking bother," I mutter, walking out.

* * *

Up at the studio Luke's sitting in a circle with a few of his dickhead mates, rapping and drinking gin from a plastic bottle.

"Where's Rapley?" I ask. They all stop and look at me.

"Gone to the food court," Luke says.

"Man, I can't believe he eats there."

"Maybe he likes the taste of roaches."

I get out my paints and start finishing up the portrait of Zlata.

"It looks heaps like her," says Luke.

"Is that your missus?" asks a small kid with a face covered in freckles.

"Yeah, maybe."

"He punched her friend," says Luke.

"Oh, at the rich girl's house? I heard about that."

"Look what I racked," Luke says, holding up a giant hunting knife.

"What you want that for?" I ask.

"Just in case."

"Don't be a fucking idiot, get rid of that thing."

* * *

Rapley's back, eating some grey meat out of a plastic container with his big sausage fingers.

"How's your day?" he asks.

"Shit so far, kicked off the sickness."

"So? You got money."

"I know. You see some of them DMT toys went over the piece behind the supermarket?"

"Serious?"

"According to Jamil."

"Motherfuckers," Rapley says, then turns to face the crowd of kids standing in the corner.

"What you fools doing?" he asks with a mouthful of meat.

"Nothing."

"Crimes," says Freckles, getting a dirty look from Luke.

"You been working on your music?" he asks Luke sternly.

"Nah, not really," Luke mumbles, looking at the ground.

"You need to do that. You're not going be young forever." Luke's face turns red.

"There. It's done," I say, stepping back from the painting.

"Looks good, man," Rapley says nodding his head.

"I'm going to give it to her tonight. She's playing downstairs."

"Good luck." Rapley chucks another piece of meat in his mouth.

58 ZLATA

MY MOTHER WAS a socialist, my father was a businessman. It sounds like a Billy Bragg song. They met at a protest against nuclear testing. In the '70s even capitalists hated the bomb. Somehow they stayed together; my mother always said it kept things lively. A few years ago they moved up north into a house with solar power.

My mother was the one who encouraged me to play music. She said it was important to have an outlet for the rage that life will breed in your heart. That you have to get it out or it'll fester, leaving you sick and bitter. She bought me my first guitar when I was seven and taught me Velvet Underground songs. I used to play them to my younger brother. "I don't know how I feel about an eight-year-old singing 'Heroin'," my father once said.

Music quickly became my life. In my teens I played in punk bands, but grew tired of being one of three women allowed on stage in that scene dominated by self-important boys. So I left behind that community of middle-class angst and started writing my own songs.

I began setting my stories to music, taking the mundane and trying to make it beautiful and important. I constructed poetry out of the fleeting loves and minor tragedies of my life, that, like dreams, were interesting only to me. With the right chords and turns of phrase I found that these personal musings became universal. For a long time I barely played any shows, just recorded in my bedroom over drum loops, building up my technique and confidence. Then Alice started seeing someone who DJed on the student radio station. One drunken night on their verandah I played him a couple of songs. A week later he emailed me asking if I had recordings. One got on the playlist and I started being offered more shows than I could play. It really seemed like things were heading somewhere. Then I got a job.

I know I told you a hundred times, but the painting you gave me was amazing. I've never really understood art. Sometimes I see something that I like but I couldn't say why. But this was beautiful. It's such a gift, being able to show people how you see them. You know that, right? I was always jealous of your talent. Music is merely approximating your feelings with notes and word-play.

* * *

When I got off stage that night you were waiting for me by the bar, looking sheepish. I had seen you come in while I was playing and fucked up one of the lines. I decided then and there that I would forgive you.

"Hey," you said, looking up at me, your head still facing the ground.

"Come here." I pulled you into me and held you. I

pulled away and ran my hand over your face. "Please don't lie to me again. It's boring."

"Okay. I got something for you."

"Really, a present?"

"Yeah, upstairs in my studio."

"You have a studio?"

"Yep."

You took my hand and led me up onto the street. The night was angry. People stumbled past us, bleeding and screaming vomit onto the footpath. A car full of teenagers raced past, all of them yelling and giving us the fingers. In the distance a bell rang out and the sound of breaking glass echoed through the streets.

"Hamish, you faggot!" A round-faced boy leered at us from a bench. He had a bag of oranges on his lap, peeling one after another and eating them. Sitting next to him was a lanky man with a cap over his eyes and a pedo moustache. I heard you sigh before walking over.

"Hey," you said, slapping both their hands. I put mine out; the tall guy just stared at it while the short one got up and gave me the same handshake. He had soft, sticky skin.

"Hello, hello." His voice was nasally and made me shiver.

"This is Zlata. This is Jamil and Skam."

"Pleased to meet you."

"Yo."

"Hey, guys," I said weakly.

"Wanna buy a phone?" the tall one asked. I saw he had blood on his shirt.

"Yeah, it's new," said Jamil, biting into an orange, juice running from his full pink lips.

"Nah, I'm good."

"I need to get some shit off you tomorrow," Jamil said.

You shot me a nervous glance. "Yeah, yeah, call me."

"Okay, lover boy. Yo, if you see Sam, we weren't here." Jamil said right before spitting orange at a couple walking past.

We went through a red door and climbed a narrow staircase. It smelt like paint and piss. You unlocked another door and led me into a tiny room. Every surface was covered in graffiti. In the centre of the room sat a large wooden table littered with art supplies, beer bottles and scraps of paper. On the walls were a number of canvases; one had a towel over it.

"Okay, you ready?" you asked.

"Yes, yes, yes!"

You pulled the towel back and there I was, but it was you as well. You had painted me standing in front of a red background, wearing my Black Flag hoodie, my eyes so blue and sad. Mine and yours combined.

"Oh my god." I felt like crying. "Why didn't you tell me you could paint like this?"

"It's nothing special."

"What do you mean?!" I hugged you. "It's incredible."

You smiled so wide.

"Really?"

"Yes, and I'm not just saying that because you made me look beautiful."

"You are beautiful."

Then we were both blushing and smiling and there was nothing else to do but kiss.

57 HAMISH

"**D**ID YOU HEAR about the American?" Sam asks. We're sitting outside some café on K road.

"No, what happened?"

"He got robbed again."

"I haven't met him."

"He's been robbed twice now. Everyone says it was Skam and Jamil."

"I saw them last night."

"Were they trying to sell a phone?"

"Yeah."

"Motherfuckers. I knew it was them."

Sam's a few years younger than me. She's in a band called Fuck Yous. It started as a joke but they've managed to make a career out of annoying people and getting drunk. They signed to a small label in the States, toured there a few times. Sam's short with an angry face and arms speckled in purposefully bad tattoos. She looks 16 but is at least 24. Her hair's a matted mess — the roots black, the rest peroxide blonde, dresses like she doesn't give a fuck but you can tell she does.

"I heard you trashed some rich girl's house," she says.

"Nah, I just punched some dick."

"That's not what Jamil said."

"Why the fuck would you listen to him?"

"It's a good story."

"I've been seeing this girl, Zlata."

"Is she rich?"

"Not really. She's cool though, has her shit together."

Sam pours her glass of water on the footpath, pulls a can of beer out of her handbag, refills the glass.

"So you're not seeing fuckface any more?"

"Me and Celia broke up last year."

"Three things I hated about her."

"Don't start this again."

"One, she wore that ugly brown mini-skirt …"

"Please."

"Two, she always had a look on her face like she needed to take a shit …"

I can't help laughing.

"Three, she used the word 'peeps' …"

"I don't know why you hate her so much, she was always real nice to you."

"Everyone's nice to me, I'm very personable."

"You can't talk anyway. What about you and that pretend junkie you were fucking last month?"

"We weren't fucking. We were making love."

We both crack up laughing.

"What you doing now?" she asks.

"Nothing."

"Want to come on the radio with me? Got to do an interview for the show tonight."

"I'll come up, but I'm not talking."

"Whatever."

* * *

Walking through the university, we're swamped by kids clutching books. Most are smiling and talking loudly, like deaf people. Sam's barely five feet tall but she manages to clear a path, swearing and shoving her way through. We climb two flights of stairs to get to the station and arrive at the reception out of breath.

"Here for the interview," Sam pants to the mousey girl with a Dead Moon T-shirt.

"What band are you in?"

"Fuck Yous."

The girl smirks. "I'll go see if the DJ's ready."

"Fucking bitch, laughing at me," Sam mutters as we sit on the couch.

* * *

The presenter's a tall blonde woman with a big, toothy smile. Soon as she talks I recognise her voice. She welcomes us in as we sit around the desk.

"Okay, guys, we're going to be on in 30 seconds."

Sam puts on a fucked-up pair of headphones, shoves another into my hands.

"I don't want them."

"You won't be able to hear yourself."

"I'm not gonna talk."

"Yes, you fucking …"

"Okay, so as promised we have Sam, drummer from Fuck Yous in the studio with us and …"

The woman looks at me and all I can see is teeth. I'm

not going to speak. I feel myself going red. Sam is staring at me with a stupid grin. The woman waves her hand for me to say something.

"Ummm, I'm not … in the band."

"Oh, okay … well, welcome anyway."

"He's my brother," Sam says. "He votes for National."

The blonde woman's smile starts to fail.

"So you guys went to South by Southwest this year. How was it?"

"Shit. Too many fucking Americans."

"You must have seen some good bands though."

"Nah, I took too much coke and had an episode."

"Oh dear. Well, the album's doing good."

"Yeah, I'm fucking rich now. I can buy my conservative brother lunch whenever."

"I'm not a National voter," I mumble into the mic.

"Nah, he's not, he's a police informant."

"Don't fucking say that."

"NARK!" yells Sam.

"Okay, so you have a gig tonight." The woman's smile's gone now. She is doing something weird with her hands.

"Oh yeah, at Whammy, it's going to be CHOICE!"

"Okay folks, so go check out Fuck Yous at Whammy tonight."

"Yeah boy!" Sam yells.

The woman with the teeth starts playing a song.

56 ZLATA

WE LAY IN BED drinking red wine from the bottle. It was raining. We whispered, despite the fact I lived alone.

"Do you sell drugs?" I was in your arms, my face buried in your chest. I always loved the way you smelt.

"Yes." You squeezed me, maybe worried I would try to leave. You thought me more innocent than I was.

"Is that how you know Christina?"

"Yeah, she's one of my customers."

We lay like that, listening to the rain for a long time.

"Hey," you said softly, breaking the silence. "Sorry I wasn't straight up with you."

"It's okay."

"I was just worried you'd freak out."

My head hurt from too much wine. I went and got some water.

"Do you want to hear my new song?" I asked when I returned.

"Yes," you said, your voice filled with genuine excitement.

"Good, because otherwise you'd have to walk home in the rain." I picked up the guitar. "I wrote it after the party, so you know …" You nodded and lay back as I began to play.

Afterwards you were silent for a bit until I shoved you.

"I like your songs, they're like stories," you said, still looking up at the mouldy ceiling.

"Yeah, I like to pretend it's therapeutic."

"Say what?"

"That they're good for you."

"True."

I sank back into the bed, our limbs reaching for each other. Something about you being a criminal excited me and I hated myself for it.

"Do you have any more secrets you want to share?" I asked.

"Not tonight."

"You're not a murderer or a spy?"

"I don't think so."

"That's a shame, it would turn me on if you were a spy," I said, climbing on top of you.

* * *

The next morning I was running late. I ate a yoghurt for breakfast on the bus, spilling half of it down the front of my skirt. I wiped it off with my hand while a teenage boy in a grey uniform stared at me. I smiled and looked out the window. I was 15 minutes late for work, but I felt good about talking to you the night before.

"What happened to your skirt?" my workmate Amber asked. I shrugged and pushed past her.

I fell into my chair and went on the internet. I'd long since given up trying to hide the fact I wasn't working. I desperately wanted to be fired but was too scared to leave of my own accord.

There was a message from Hayley.

"So, turns out your violent bf is also selling drugs to my sister."

"You're a stripper who pretends they're from money. Empathy, Hayley, empathy," I typed. As soon as I sent it, I was filled with anxiety. We didn't talk about her job unless she brought it up, let alone make fun of her for it.

"I hope that's work-related," Amber said as she strode past with an armful of papers.

"Of course it is," I called after her.

* * *

Hayley rang up, furious, just before lunch.

"What the fuck?" she said. "I'm trying to look out for you."

"I know, I'm sorry."

"I don't want you to get fucked around again."

"Well, that's kind of my problem, isn't it?"

"It usually ends up my problem too."

"I don't want to argue. Let's get a drink tomorrow." I could hear her stewing on the other end. She wanted to keep fighting.

"Okay, Zlata, let's meet at that new wine bar on Ponsonby Road."

I rolled my eyes. "Sure thing."

55 HAMISH

"SO IT'S BACK ON with you and Zlata?" Rapley asks. We're standing by that wall behind the supermarket. There's a big red line spray-painted through both our pieces.

"Yeah, told her everything the other night."

"Happy for you, you deserve someone nice."

There's a couple of sloppy DMT throw-ups on the wall. Stupid kids trying to get a name.

"What's been up with you?" I ask.

"Same old, been seeing Kate."

We both stare at the wall in silence for a bit.

"So we doing this show? It's going to be at a proper gallery. Might make some cash," Rapley says.

"I don't think so."

Rapley smiles. I think about the show. I hate the idea of looking stupid in front of all those people with their education and money.

"I'm going to kill these motherfuckers," Rapley says as we walk off.

* * *

Me and Zlata are on our way to the movies. She likes films I've never heard of from countries I didn't know existed.

"Have you travelled much?" she asks. I laugh.

"I went to the South Island for this painting thing."

"You've never been overseas?"

"Nah, you?"

"Yeah. I've been a few places. I saved up after uni, my folks helped me out too."

"What's the best country you've been to?"

"Probably Spain, or maybe Cuba."

"That's crazy, what was it like in Cuba?"

"Hot, confusing, beautiful."

"Like you."

"So charming." She kisses me. "Oh, I got something for you." She reaches into her bag and hands me a book. "Now you can better yourself."

I look at the cover, *Postmodernism for Beginners*.

"Thanks." I open it and see three words I don't know in the first sentence.

"Don't make that face when someone gives you a lovely gift."

"What face?"

"Like you just bit into a lemon."

"No, it's cool. I just haven't read anything since forever."

* * *

It's Tuesday I think. I'm at the bus stop, trying to read the fucking book. The bus is twenty minutes late. Trying to keep calm. I have to meet Jamil in town to sell him some shit. I read the same sentence for the third time. This is so confusing.

"Hamish." Mark's walking over. He's dressed weird, in a fancy shirt, his hair done nice but his jeans have a giant rip in the crotch.

"What's up, why you dressed like that?"

"Had court today." He's tall, always shuffles from one foot to the other like some kind of dance.

"What for?"

"Got busted with weed."

"How'd it go?"

"Got convicted but not going inside."

"You wore that?"

"Yeah, could only afford a shirt."

"But your jeans have a hole in them."

"These are my good jeans."

"Should have borrowed some, man. They won't let you travel now."

"Like I was going to travel anyway." He looks around quickly like someone might be sneaking up on him.

"True."

"What you reading?"

"*Postmodernism for Beginners.*"

"Give us a look."

I hand him the book. He flicks through it.

"Out of it. You understand all this?"

"Not really."

"Heard you and Rapley are doing a show," he says, tossing the book back to me.

"Maybe, we'll see."

"You should, it'd be mean."

Out of the corner of my eye I see the bus.

"This is me."

"All right, take care."

"You too."

I get on the bus, fighting the urge to punch the driver for being so fucking late. Up the back I take out a Posca and start writing 'sex' over and over again on the back of the seat.

54 ZLATA

I WAS LATE to meet Hayley. I sat in the back of a cab, thinking of excuses. I had one but she wouldn't understand.

I'd woken up early to find you already gone on some mysterious errand. After a breakfast of baked beans and coffee I decided to clean the house. The floor was covered in clothes, the dishes were filthy and the place stank. I opened the windows and spent an hour picking things up, constantly distracted by the need to annoy people on the internet. By 11 the place didn't really look much different but I was sick of cleaning. I sat on the couch, tagging Hayley in photos of old people. She had a phobia of the elderly. When this grew dull I headed up to the supermarket. The house was stripped bare of food.

I was feeling more anxious than usual that morning, but put it down to being hungover. I walked past the Tongan church where a choir was singing and turned up the music on my phone, the sweet harmonies mixing with the sounds of Americans yelling about money.

Heading home, I decided to walk past the house where I grew up. The bags cut into my hands as I walked towards the street. Since my parents sold it five years ago it had had several owners, each one doing a little work and selling it for increasingly ridiculous prices. I liked looking at the new renovations every so often. Last time, they had cut down all the trees and turned the tall corrugated iron fence into a small picket one.

Sometimes I remember the house fondly, summers endless and burning, running with my brother through the streets until we were dragged inside, me and my mother filling the house with music till it poured out from the doors and windows. Other times it is cold and dark, the winter refusing to leave, my parents arguing about money, coming home to find a window broken and everything stolen or smashed time and again.

I turned down my old street, singing a loud duet with my phone when I tripped and almost lost my balance. At first I thought my foot had slipped. Then I realised that the footpath was loose. I looked up and two houses away from my old place the concrete began to crack and fall away into a dark hole in the ground. I stood there watching the footpath crumble like sand, the hole opening up before me in a giant yawn. Only when the mouth had almost reached my feet did I turn and run.

* * *

I woke up with a jolt, it was late afternoon. I sat up in bed and grabbed a half-empty bottle of wine, my hands shaking. I popped another of my anti-anxiety pills and finished the wine. I tried to ring you again but your phone was off. You never checked your voicemail. I hung up and lay in bed staring at the black mould on the ceiling. I needed you but you were off selling drugs or vandalising things. At some point the phone beeped. I grabbed at it frantically but it was only Hayley.

"Where are you?" I had completely forgotten our meeting. I leapt up and changed into a dress and put on deodorant. I felt tired and disgusting. I decided against taking my chances with the bus and called a cab. I was glad it was Saturday. I wanted to get drunk.

* * *

"Finally," Hayley said when I arrived. She was seated at a small iron table with a half-empty bottle of wine. She had a black shirt done up to her neck and her hair was pulled back in a tight ponytail. She looked intense and would have intimidated me if I didn't know her secrets. I walked over, swaying slightly from the mix of Valium and wine.

The age difference in the bar between men and women was about 15 years in favour of the women. I hated the place immediately. Music for people who don't like music hung in the background. It depressed me that this suffocating atmosphere was what these people considered relaxing. I thought about how much you would have loathed that place and it made me miss you even more.

"Look how much I had to drink by myself."

"Don't worry, I've already had a bottle."

"What's wrong?"

"Nothing."

"Are you having panic attacks again?"

"No, just tired." I sat down and poured myself a large glass.

"Have you been taking your pills?"

"Yes," I snapped.

"You hungry? They have nice tapas here," Hayley said, ignoring my outburst.

"No thanks, I had a sandwich before." We sat in silence while I took long gulps of wine, trying to stave off my headache.

"I'm sorry about that message the other day."

"It's okay." Hayley said warmly, and I felt bad for being so harsh on her.

"I know you're just worried about me."

"Look, if Hamish makes you happy then that's all that's important really."

"He does. I mean, I know how he looks on paper, but he's really kind."

"Yeah. Christina was singing his praises."

We both laugh.

"Jesus, it does sound bad when she's someone's character reference."

"Maybe he's good at his job," Hayley said, still laughing.

We drank the rest of the bottle. I wanted to tell Hayley about the footpath and the house, but I knew she would get upset and we were having a good time.

"What's the sex like?" Hayley asked loudly. I felt my cheeks turn red.

"It's good."

"Is he into that rough shit, like you?"

"No, but I like it, it's a change. He's really gentle."

"I went home with this guy the other night. He tried to choke me so I kneed him in the balls."

"No!"

"Yep, that's not for me," she said, leaning back in her chair. "Do you have plans this evening?"

"Nah, I got the day off tomorrow so maybe keep drinking."

"You're not working tomorrow?"

"It's Sunday tomorrow."

"It's Sunday now."

"Ahh shit. Really?"

"Yeah, babe," Hayley said, looking concerned.

53 HAMISH

"WE SHOULD GO visit my parents one day."
Zlata's lying naked on the bed, playing with one
of my markers.

We're listening to The Smiths, smoking some shitty
weed I found under my bed. Bella and Jean are fucking
loudly in the next room. I turn up the music.

"They're really going for it," Zlata giggles.

"Every fucking night."

I'm sketching Rapley's old pit bull from memory. I can't
get the nose right.

"My mum really wants to meet you," she says.

"Serious?"

"Of course, baby."

I don't usually get along with people's parents. My
first serious girlfriend's father beat the shit out of me
when he caught me in bed with his daughter. Then there
was the time me and Rapley accidentally stole Celia's
mum's car.

"They have an amazing house up north. You'd like it there."

I don't say anything, just keep drawing.

I can feel her watching me.

"Does your mum still live across the park?"

"Yeah."

"When was the last time you saw her?"

I put the pen down and try to remember. It was one Christmas, me and her in that damp house drinking till we had an argument about some shit and I stormed out.

"Don't know. Two or three years ago."

She reaches out and strokes my face. I know she's trying to be kind but it makes me feel weak.

"Rapley's asked me to do a show with him." I try to change the subject.

"Oh, baby, that's so cool."

"I don't know if I'm ready."

"Of course you are, your work is so good."

"You think?"

"Yes, I love what you do."

"I feel like I'm always in his shadow, ya know." I fuck the nose up again. "I can't even draw a dog." I laugh.

"I wouldn't worry, I can't play a proper F major and look at me."

* * *

I can't sleep. Zlata's got me thinking about Mum now. I feel shitty for never going round there, but all we do is fight about the past. Zlata rolls over and puts her arms round me.

"Do you think about getting out of here?" she whispers in the dark.

"Yeah, nah, sometimes."

"Where would you like to go?"

"I don't know, what 'bout you?"

"Iceland," she says.

"Where's that?"

"As far away as you can get from here."

52 ZLATA

AFTER THREE MONTHS we had found a routine; a dance between day and night. We moved gracefully from one life to the next, never letting the sun throw the moon off time. Mostly I didn't think about how you made your money or why you came home bruised and cut. Though we shared a bed and a neighbourhood, we inhabited different worlds. We measured out the pieces of the day that made the other half bearable: art, music, dancing, drinking, fucking. We kept the rest locked behind doors the other didn't know existed.

I wrote a lot of new songs around that time. Of course they were about you and your crazy life, but I denied it. I was embarrassed to have become one of those musicians who churns out love songs. In the past I always had a level of detachment in my music, giving the listener a wink or a wry smile when things got too heavy. But love made that approach seem disingenuous.

I booked some studio time with a friend who had a good home set-up. I wanted to capture the new songs before they grew old. There is nothing worse than losing a song to time. Though they are the children of memories, they age differently. Even the most traumatic event can make for a good story with enough time as a buffer. But a song doesn't become funnier or more poignant as the years pile up. They are sickly creatures; turn your back for a second and they're gone.

* * *

I arrived at Matt's apartment on Symonds Street with my guitar and a flash drive filled with backing tracks. Matt was tall and thin with a yellowish hue. He claimed this was from lack of sunlight, but it was more likely the amount of homemade spirits he consumed.

"Morning," I said when he opened the door, his eyes sleepy, his hair a mess.

"Is it? I thought it was the afternoon."

"No, it's like 10, isn't it?" I checked my phone and saw it was 2 p.m. "Fuck."

"Don't worry, I only just woke up."

I followed him into his house. His flat was a mess of bottles and green rubbish bins, which he used to concoct his evil-tasting liquor.

Guitars of various makes were leaning everywhere. In the corner of the living room was a laptop with a dozen leads emerging from it.

"New songs?" he asked.

"Yeah, all of them."

"You've been productive."

I unpacked my guitar while Matt began to set up mics.

"So, I hear you've been seeing Hamish?"

"You know him?"

"Yeah, we went to school together. His friend Rapley is doing my band's album cover."

"Small world."

"Small town."

* * *

Over two days we laid down six songs. They came out really strong. Matt was good at pointing out, in an encouraging way, the parts that sucked. "You know how you go out of time in that line — what do you think it would sound like if you didn't?"

At the end of the session we sat on the corner of his street, drinking beer.

"What was Hamish like at school?" I asked.

"Pretty loose. We got along, but he was nuts."

"Really?"

"Yeah, him and Rapley. I like him, but he's crazy." Matt finished his beer. "Anyway, I'm sure he's changed."

He left the bottle on the street and walked back inside.

I sat there and looked at the view. Streets snaked through the valley, each one paved with 28 years of memories. It felt like if you followed the right one you could pick up where things started to go wrong. But the truth was every one of those roads led to dead ends.

51 HAMISH

TIMOTHY'S OUT FRONT of his house, wearing nothing but a Batman mask.

"Yo." He's silent, staring with his crazy brown eyes. "Is Mum home?"

Slowly he starts backing away, then turns and sprints inside. The sounds of drums and guitar are coming from the house. Inside, the music's deafening. I cover my ears. Sam's playing the drums. Louisa strums her blood-red guitar like she hates it. On the couch, Timothy and his two younger sisters sit staring at me. I wait until the song falls apart. Sam throws the drumsticks down and storms out the room. Louisa's laughing.

"You put us off," she says, unplugging her guitar, kissing me on the cheek, her voice scratchy and warm.

"Sorry."

"Want some cake?" Sam yells from the kitchen.

"What kind is it?"

"I don't know. It's orange."

"Okay."

The two sisters pick up the discarded sticks and start banging on the drums.

"Come out the back," Louisa yells over the noise.

* * *

We sit under the lemon tree. Someone's hammered animal masks into the trunk. They watch us as Louisa opens a beer. She takes a sip and passes it to me. She's one of the only people I know who has her shit together. Well, I mean she's always well dressed and hardly ever cries in public.

"How you been?" she says, smiling.

"Good, busy as."

"I heard you're seeing the girl from Picnic."

"Yeah, been a few months."

"She's cool, we did some shows with her a while back. She's pretty straight, right?"

"Yeah, I guess."

"That's nice though. You don't always have to go out with crazies."

Sam walks outside holding a plate with the orange cake on it. Timothy follows behind her, naked, still wearing the mask.

"There's enough of them around," she laughs.

The cake hasn't been cut so I rip some off with my hands.

"It's nice. It's from the supermarket," Sam pulls a piece off and gives it to Timothy. He snatches it, runs back inside. I can still hear the sound of the drums being slowly destroyed.

"What's news?" Sam asks.

The cake tastes like shit.

"Just talking about Zlata."

"You still with her? I thought she dumped you after you smashed up her mate's house."

"That never happened."

"Yeah, I heard about that," Louisa says, picking off little bits of cake.

"Just rumours."

"Well, it's nice you've found someone who can stomach you," Sam says. She rolls up the sleeves on her Misfits T-shirt and lies back, her hands behind her head.

"What about you?" I ask. "Still hanging around the American?"

Louisa shouts with laughter, sending bits of cake flying all over her long white dress.

"Shut up," Sam says hitting her on the arm.

"What? Did he get robbed again?"

"No, he broke his arm."

"How?"

Sam goes silent, looking at the ground. It's the first time I've ever seen her lost for words.

"Can I tell him?" Louisa asks gleefully.

"Whatever."

"He had a rollerblading accident."

"Bullshit," I say.

"He did, he did."

"I didn't know he rollerbladed," Sam says quietly.

"I feel like I don't know you any more," I say, ripping off another piece of cake.

"Fuck up."

"So, you going to start rollerblading too?"

"Seriously, someone is going to get kicked in the nuts in a minute."

Me and Sam are walking down Great North Road. It's hot and I forgot my sunglasses. We're heading to the park to score weed off Dumb and Dumber. Because Sam's short and always on her phone, I have to keep waiting for her to catch up.

"Who're you texting?"

"No one."

"Is it the inline skater?"

"No, it's not the American."

"How many boyfriends do you have?"

"Enough."

We cut down Turakina Street.

"Hey, I was going to ask if you could help Zlata out."

"She want a haircut?"

"What? No, I mean with her music."

"I'll cut her hair."

"Maybe give her demos to your label."

"She'd look nice with an undercut."

It's late afternoon when we get to the park. Jamil and Skam are nowhere to be seen. Some teenagers play basketball on the half court; children climb on the playground like ants. "They said they'd be here," I say, surveying the field. "Let's grab a six."

We buy a six-pack of VB from the dairy. Back at the park, we sit up on the half pipe in a lazy silence. The only noise is the kids, and us sipping our beers.

"How's Rapley?" Sam asks.

"He's all good. His new shit's mean."

"Yeah, his art's always good."

"He asked me to do a show with him."

"You going to?"

"Maybe."

"You should, you idiot."

"Do you think so?"

"The fuck else you going to do?"

"Thanks."

"You know what I mean."

A guy I recognise from around turns up with a skateboard. He gives me a nod before dropping in, gliding up and down the ramp, cutting through the golden light. We sit watching, lost in his style.

"Hey, faggots." The skater loses his balance and falls hard on his back. I turn and see Skam and Jamil walking towards us. Me and Sam both sigh and slide down the ramp.

50 ZLATA

KARANGAHAPE ROAD, WHERE the studio was, used to be the red-light district of Auckland. Then it became more of a red-light block. The few remaining sex stores relegated to one end of the street, curiosities from a time before the internet and soaring rents. As children, our family would sometimes drive down K Rd at night. I remember looking at the sex workers who stood in the shadows, even then, wanting to know their stories. The strip clubs had photos of naked women out front that you could just glimpse as the car sped past. At the time none of this seemed sleazy; like the sudden storms of conflict, the nights that echoed with cries and laughter or the adults lost in waking dreams, it was just how things were. Most night life within central Auckland revolved around this one street. The handful of venues and bars worth visiting were located there. On the weekends the street filled with drag queens and drug addicts, hipsters and homeless, streetwalkers and suburbanites, all drinking and screaming for love or, at the very least, sex. Come morning, these weekend Cinderellas would stagger home, leaving the streets empty except for the odd glass slipper, blood stains and broken bottles.

I spent a lot of time up in your studio. It was on my way home from work and I enjoyed the noise and chaos that followed you around. All that energy inspired me and distracted me from my anxieties. After a few weeks me and Rapley were getting along well. Though I wouldn't have wanted any of my friends to date him he had a good heart and looked out for you. I liked to smoke weed and sit on the window ledge looking out over the street, watching familiar faces going about their lives. The strangest thing about that place was the music. Aside from hip hop, it was country and old folk records playing on that beat-up computer.

And of course there was the constant coming and going of visitors: young people who looked up to you, using the studio as somewhere to get high and drink; other artists who came and swapped ideas and drugs; musicians who hung out before playing at the venue downstairs; older people whose relationship to you and Rapley I was never quite sure of. Everyone was always welcomed, if not with open arms then at least with a "Hey bro" and a slap of the hand. None of these interruptions slowed either of you down. In fact, they all seemed to serve a purpose in the creating of your art. People would be sent to fetch booze, food or drugs, musicians would play songs and everyone always told stories. They could all tell a good tale; from the 15-year-old overweight girl who stole Red Bulls out of the fridge to the old junkie guy who sold painkillers. These stories of disaster and lunacy were always spoken with good humour no matter how tragic the outcome, repeated over and over, until they became finely honed fables, legends of the central city.

49 HAMISH

"HAVE YOU FINISHED the book yet?" Zlata asks. We're holding hands, walking up Williamson Ave.

"Nah, not yet. I'm like maybe a quarter in."

"But it's such a short book," she laughs kindly.

"I know." It's a hot evening, despite the trees blocking out the last of the sun. We're off to meet Rapley and his new love interest at some bar on K Road.

Zlata's in a green summer dress. Her hair's tied back, her face glows, she looks beautiful.

"Sam, Louisa and that are heading to Coromandel soon. Wanna come?"

"I guess. I mean, will it be okay?"

"Will what be okay?"

"I don't really know them."

"Of course. Lou's choice, Sam's nuts but she's cool."

"Okay, let's do it." She claps her hands.

* * *

The place is full of bike riders in stupid lycra outfits and funny shoes. We find Rapley and Kate at the bar.

"Hey," Rapley says, getting up and hugging me.

"Zlata," he says, slapping her hand.

"This is Kate."

I think I've met her before but can't remember where. She's short with light brown skin and beautiful watery eyes. She looks too exotic to be hanging out in this dump.

"Hey," I say, giving her an awkward hug.

"Hello. Gosh, you're stunning," says Zlata, throwing her arms round her.

"Hey guys," she mumbles.

"Let's grab a booth," Rapley says, pushing past a couple of bike riders.

"So what's up with the show?" Rapley asks me.

"What's this?" Kate says.

"We're doing an art show together."

"That's so cool."

"I don't know," I say, pulling the label off my beer.

"You have to do it," Zlata says.

"See? If your best mate and your girlfriend's telling you to do something, you should listen." I look up. Everyone's staring. My face goes red.

"Okay, fuck it, I'll do it."

"All right!" yells Rapley, slapping the table, making the bike riders turn and stare.

"Now, all we need's a cool name."

"*A Couple of Handsomes Make Some Art*?" Zlata says.

"I hope your songs are better than your show titles."

"You should hear them," I say. "They're real cool." Zlata smiles at me.

"You make music?" Kate asks.

"Yeah, sometimes."

"Wow, you guys are all so talented."

"We should go to the studio and listen to them," I say.

"They're not really finished."

"If I'm doing this art show, you can play your demos."

* * *

We're all sitting round at the studio when Sam bursts in.

"Okay, first thing, this place fucking stinks," she says, throwing her leather jacket on the table. "Have you losers been pissing in here again?"

"Hello, everyone," says Louisa, following behind Sam.

"Sam, Lou, this is Kate."

"You're a babe," says Sam, still holding her nose.

"Thanks," says Kate, her cheeks turning red. I'm bent over the computer.

"Can we please, please, please not listen to depressing redneck music?" says Sam. "It's been a long week."

"It's only Tuesday."

"Exactly."

"Anyway, we're here to listen to Zlata's new demos."

"That's right, I forgot to tell you," says Louisa, "Sam talked to the dude at the label and he knows who you are and he wants to hear the demos."

"Really?" says Zlata, "That's so nice of you."

"He asked us to," Sam says, pointing at me.

"Okay, shut up. I'm pressing play."

48 ZLATA

THE MONTHS LEADING UP to the art show were some of the most exciting and exhausting of my life. It was summer, everyone was focused and happy. I met with the label, they liked the demos and there was talk of an album. I worked into the night on new songs, turning up to work exhausted and late. Fire me, I screamed throughout the day, but no one listened, so I wrote a song about it. Fuck Yous had just got a deal in Europe and a big tour was planned. The world was still falling to pieces around us. Nothing seemed to work how it should. The power went out every other day, sirens wailed at night like terrified babies, bodies filled the harbour. But for a time we had a respite from collapse, a brief holiday in our collective passions. The studio was even more alive than usual; everyone came together to rally behind their friends. We were champions going into battle, telling our stories to the outside world. We all walked proud for those short months.

I started hanging out with the weird kid, Luke. We would sit up in the studio with our guitars while the others painted. He only knew three chords and changed them round, endlessly making up songs that alternated between genius and moronic. I taught him some technique and he quickly improved.

"You're a brilliant idiot," I once told him. A wide smile filled his gaunt face.

I began to notice that he was always the last to leave the studio or the party or the gig. When I asked him why he never wanted to go home, he simply shrugged. Rapley told me he lived with his mother in a falling down house in Morningside.

"She's a bit fucked in the head," he said, sadly.

You loved Luke. One of the few times you'd drop the nihilistic façade you wore in public was when he needed you. For a week he slept on your floor while his mother was in the psych ward. You brought him clothes and food and scared off anyone who might wish to hurt him. The dysfunction of your families forced you to create your own. And while it was one riddled with substance abuse and anxiety, its heart was filled with love.

* * *

I also became close with Louisa. I started going round to her house a lot, we drank and played music while her wild children danced and destroyed the furniture.

When I told my mum about everything she was more excited about my new friends than the record deal. She had been in a band that had had some success in the '80s and was always offering me advice.

"Honey, a community like that is so much more valuable than any record deal," she gushed in her slight accent. "I'm so excited. And the new songs you sent me are brilliant."

"Thanks, Mum."

"Are they about Hayden?"

"Hamish. Yeah, I guess."

"Well, it seems you've found your muse."

"I miss you."

"I miss you too, Bubs. When are you going to come and visit?"

"Soon."

"You have to bring Hayden."

"Hamish, Mum."

"Yes, him too."

But then there was the rent. I was already paying half my wages for the privilege of living in a shitty apartment on Rose Road. One day a letter came saying it was going up another $50 a week. Even with work and what I made at shows, this would have left me hopelessly broke. I met Hayley and Alice for coffee and told them of my predicament.

"You should just move to the 'burbs," said Hayley. Though it was only 3 p.m., she looked tired.

"No, thanks. Imagine having to commute an hour to and from work every day."

"Well, maybe you could work out of the city."

"So basically just never see anyone."

"We should just move to Australia with everyone else," Alice said excitedly.

"That place is so dull," Hayley said, "If you're going to uproot your life you may as well go further."

"Laos," said Alice, a smile lifting her red cheeks.

"What?"

"We should move to Laos, it's amazing."

"You're doing that thing again," Hayley snapped.

"What thing?"

"When you ruin conversations by talking nonsense."

"I'm not," said Alice, pouting and looking away.

"Thanks, but maybe I'll just stick it out and see what happens with the record deal."

"Oh, that's exciting," said Alice.

"Yeah, if it happens."

"I'm glad someone's finally taking notice of you," said Hayley, finishing her coffee. "You should have been famous years ago."

"You're a bit famous. I saw someone wearing one of your T-shirts at the library."

"Is it too early to drink?" Hayley asked. "Of course it isn't," she answered herself, waving aggressively at the waiter.

* * *

Later that night I stumbled up to the studio. Nebraska blared out of the open door. It was past midnight but I was still surprised to find you up there alone, working on another portrait of me.

"Hello, sexy," I said, making you jump.

"Fuck," you said, laughing. "You gave me a fright."

"Where is everyone?"

"Rapley's off with Kate. Everyone else has gone to that party."

"Whose party?"

"I don't know." I walked up and hugged you. I loved

your body, strong with a layer of fat that made you good for cuddling. "I'm drunk."

"I can tell," you said, going back to your painting.

I studied the canvas. Again you had given me your eyes. You never told me if it was a conscious decision.

"My rent is going up again."

"How much money do they fucking need?"

"I don't think I can afford to keep living there."

"Move in with me," you said, still painting.

"Really?"

You put your brush down and turned to face me. "Yeah, it'd be fun." You started stroking my hair.

I pulled a beer out of my handbag and popped it open on the side of the table. It was warm and burnt my throat. I hadn't thought about moving in with you, but it made sense.

"What about all my stuff?"

"There's enough room."

"Okay, fuck it, why not."

"I'll ask Bella tomorrow. I reckon she'll be sweet with it."

"So are all the paintings going to be of me?" I asked, passing you the beer.

"Maybe." You took a sip. "Ahhh, this is warm," you said, and spat it on the ground.

* * *

That night we stayed at your house. It was too hot for blankets so we lay naked under a thin scratchy sheet. Outside someone was screaming. Your hands moved up and down my body, stopping and squeezing my breasts, my belly, my ass, letting out little groans of pleasure. I reached for your cock.

"You're so hard," I whispered.

The screams outside grew louder as more people joined in. Your hand moved down between my legs. I loved the way you touched me, with gentle proficiency. You were rubbing me while I whispered filth in your ear.

"I want you to fuck the shit out of me … use me, choke me."

Somewhere in the distance, a window smashed.

You climbed on top of me and pushed yourself inside slowly. We both moaned as you stretched me open. I put my hand behind your neck and pulled you towards me while you moved slowly in and out. I was whispering nothings in between each lazy kiss.

"You're so special, you know that. So beautiful."

I always had to talk to keep my mind from wandering. One minute I'd be in throes of passion, the next thinking about how I needed new guitar strings.

In contrast you never said a word, almost immediately becoming lost in the act. The sound of breaking glass grew closer, people screamed and cheered, fear and celebration.

You started fucking me faster. I wrapped my legs around you. Your head was buried in the pillow next to mine. I lifted it up.

"Look at me," I said. Your eyes remained closed.

"Look at me."

You opened your eyes and we stared into each other. Without warning, I pushed you off and climbed on top of you. Placing my hands on your chest, I lifted myself up and down on your cock. I knew you liked it. Sirens joined the screams, flames danced outside the window.

"I want to come," I said. You pulled me down on top of you; your chest was wet with sweat. Holding me with one hand behind my neck the other on my back, you fucked me deep and fast until I came so hard my vision blurred. I went limp on top of you while you continued fucking me until you came. We lay there like that in the summer heat, panting and covered in each other. My legs quivered as I listened to the last screams echoing in the distance.

* * *

Later we showered, taking turns washing each other.

"I love you," you said, rubbing the soap over my breasts. It was the first time a lover had said that to me without filling me with dread.

"I love you so much," I replied.

We kissed while the warm water ran down over us, washing our past into the sewers.

47 HAMISH

W E'RE WALKING OVER Bond Street Bridge, heading to a party. Me, Rapley, Skam, Luke and Nicholas. All talking shit, excited, half pissed. I love this time of night, out with the boys, feeling like anything could happen. Every so often someone stops and tags on a sign or a lamp post. Rapley's drinking from a bottle of vodka, telling stories.

"So we were real stoned, you know when you get all twitchy and shit? And this pig walks into my room."

"A cop?" Luke asks.

"Nah bro, an actual pig, and me and Hamish are like 'What the fuck?' It just stands there looking at us for a minute and runs out."

"You serious?"

"Yeah. Turns out the neighbours were having an umu and it escaped," he laughs.

"Crazy."

"Where's Zlata tonight?" Nicholas asks.

After Luke, Nicholas is the youngest in our crew. He confuses everyone, dresses like a rich kid, talks educated and spends his time hanging out with losers like us. He started coming up to the studio one day. We thought he was just another kid with nowhere else to be, till we saw his work. Rapley was jealous at first; he's not used to being shown up. Eventually he had to accept that Nicholas is just better than him.

"She's at home, working on some music."

"I heard she's going to be on the same label as Fuck Yous."

He's got on a woollen vest over a brown shirt, his hair's blond and parted on the side. His mother's a well-known film director and his father's a writer or some shit. They have a massive house filled with books and films and love. Nicholas still lives there with his two younger sisters. Sometimes I like to visit, get high with his parents and see how good life can be.

"Yeah, I think so."

"That's so cool. I always liked her in Picnic. She has a really interesting way of telling stories; self-aware without being ironic."

"Postmodern?" I say.

Nicholas laughs.

"I guess."

* * *

At the party, people are all over the street. Little Scott the singer in this punk band comes running over.

"Hey," he cries out. He's wearing gold underwear, a cape and nothing else.

"You look fucking crazy," Luke says, laughing.

"We're playing in one minute exactly."

"Scott," someone yells, "Where the fuck are you?"

"Come and watch me!" Scott shouts, disappearing into the crowd.

Me, Luke and Nicholas follow after him. The others stay out the front greeting people, talking shit. We know pretty much everyone here. By the time we finish hugging and slapping hands with them the band's doing their second song. Scott's on stage naked — he climbs on top of an amp, tucks his dick between his legs and holds his arms out like Jesus. The song kicks in. He leaps into the crowd screaming. Everyone's going crazy. Nicholas is up the front while I hang back with Luke. The song finishes and Scott manages to pull his underpants back on.

"This is a love song," he yells into the mic. "Sing along!"

The drummer counts them in and Scott starts screaming "drugs, drugs, drugs". I look round the room. It's the usual crowd: exes, enemies, friends and acquaintances. The band starts another song but I'm bored now. I start pushing my way out when I see *them* standing in the kitchen.

I find Rapley outside talking to some girl. Skam is standing behind him with some guys I don't recognise, passing a bottle around.

"Rapley."

He looks up at me, annoyed.

"What?"

"Some of those dudes are here." Luke joins us, looking concerned.

"What dudes."

"Those toys that's been capping us."

"DMT?"

"Yeah, inside. There's three of them."

Nicholas walks over red-faced and covered in sweat.

"Man that was fun." He looks at us. "What's wrong?"

"Those DMT eggs are here," Rapley says.

"Ahh fuck, let's leave it. I'm having a good night."

"We've been after them for ages."

"So?"

"Don't be a pussy."

"Don't be a psycho."

I see them walk outside and down the back of the house with a couple of girls.

"Skam!" I yell out. He ambles over. Rapley's already following after them.

"Stay here if you want," I say to Nicholas.

"Fuck this," he says, walking back inside. Luke starts to follow us.

"Nah, you go with Nicholas," I say, pushing him towards the house. He looks like he's going to complain, but then heads inside.

* * *

Me and Skam are walking down when the two girls run past, one of them crying. Round the back someone's lying starfish on the ground, the other two are backing up against a fence.

"It wasn't us, man," one of them pleads.

"Bullshit," says Rapley, closing in. One of them swings a bottle at Rapley's head. It connects but doesn't break. Rapley punches him square in the face, making a cracking sound. The other guy tries to run past us but I catch him with a punch to the side of the head. He falls and me and Skam start kicking him in the kidneys and head.

"Stop it," he keeps crying, making me kick him harder.

Rapley's stomping the guy he just punched.

Suddenly a door swings open, throwing light onto the backyard. I look up. A wall of faces are staring at us. No one moves to come outside. I see Nicholas in the crowd, shaking his head.

"Let's go," I say, kicking the guy again in the ribs. We quickly walk back round the side of the house and leave.

46 ZLATA

I WAS FINISHING UP a new song when Hayley
arrived. She was wearing a tight black dress and black
gloves. She looked like a villain in a children's film.

"So, this is the new place?" she said, walking in and
quickly surveying the bedroom. I put my guitar back in its
case.

"I have this," she said, holding up a bottle of red wine.
"And an insatiable thirst."

"I thought you had a date tonight."

"I did. He was so fucking boring I left." We went and
sat in the kitchen, poured wine. "He kept talking about his
boat and his ex — two things I have zero interest in."

"Oh well, I'm sure you'll meet someone else."

"Of course. I have another date tomorrow night," she
said absent-mindedly, looking around the kitchen.

"So, you been here two weeks?"

"Three."

"And it's just you and Hamish."

"No, there's this girl Bella as well."

"Cosy …" We both drank our wine.

"How's work?" she asked. I felt my stomach turn.

"Like hell with all the good bits removed. How's your work?"

"It's slow. I blame internet porn and the fucking recession. Where's Hamish tonight?"

"At some party."

* * *

We had just finished the wine when you came home. Rapley and the guy with the pedo moustache walked in with you. Everyone was unusually quiet. You and Rapley sat down at the table while the tall one stood behind us, making me feel uncomfortable.

"How was your night?" I asked. Rapley forced a smile.

"It was okay," you said, without looking at me.

"Whose party was it?"

"Don't know." We sat in silence for a while.

"Well, you've really brought the party atmosphere home with you," Hayley said.

You shot her a look but she didn't notice.

"Is there any booze here?" the tall guy asked.

"Check the fridge."

You reached out and held my hand across the table and I saw that your knuckles were bleeding. Rapley's hands were as well.

Hayley caught my eye and frowned.

"Well, as much fun as this is, I'm off," she said, getting to her feet. I hugged her and she whispered, "What the fuck?" in my ear. I shrugged.

* * *

That night we inhabited different worlds in the same bed. After everyone left we argued. In the past, I'd ignored the detritus of violence you dragged home. But seeing the situation through Hayley's eyes, I realised what I was condoning. At first you denied anything happening, but you lied with a burnt tongue. Then you tried to excuse your actions, bringing up the ridiculous code you claimed to live by. I said you were behaving like a lunatic, and retreated to bed in a wake of slamming doors. I was surprised when you joined me not long after. Usually when we fought, the night would swallow you.

After lying there for an hour, I reached out and put my hand on your chest. I felt you tense.

"Are you okay?" I asked quietly. You said nothing, just lay there breathing heavily. "Baby, talk to me."

"Fuck off," you snapped, shoving me and rolling away.

This was the first time I remember being afraid of you.

* * *

The next morning I got up early and called my brother Luka.

"Can you come get me?" I whispered in the hallway. While you slept, I packed a bag and wrote you a note. *Gone to my folks for a few days — ring me when you decide you don't want to treat me like shit.* I grabbed my guitar and waited out front.

Despite feeling like I was suffocating, the morning was beautiful. Flowers forced themselves through the cracks in the road and footpath, children with clown face paint ran past holding hands, seagulls and magpies sang from the trees and the sun smiled down at me.

My brother pulled up in his beat-up red car.

"Hey, you," I said, climbing in. He smiled, his handsome face covered in a messy black beard. He reached out and gave me a squeeze on the shoulder with his calloused hands.

"You live here now?" he asked, looking through the windscreen at the house.

"Yeah."

"You okay?" His blue eyes filled with worry.

"Yeah, Luka. I just need a break."

"So I guess you're coming back to mine."

"I'm going to go stay with Mum and Dad. Can you drop me at the bus terminal?"

"If you wait till lunch I'll drive you up."

"Really?"

"Yeah, why not? I need to go see them. Jenna will be home at lunchtime. We'll head up after."

* * *

Back at Luka's house I tried to nap on the couch while his cat-sized dog, Mr Jenkins, leapt up, barking and running away.

"Fucking animal," my brother yelled, throwing a shoe at it. "Sorry."

"It's okay," I mumbled.

Jenna got home round 11.30 a.m., with a plastic bag filled with food.

"Is that Zlata?" she squealed, dropping the bag and leaping on top of me.

"Jesus," I gasped as she knocked the wind out of me. We hugged each other tightly.

"So good to see you," she said, getting back to her feet. Jenna was a small, solid woman with a disarmingly pretty face.

"You too." I sat up and stretched.

Jenna and my brother had been together since meeting in their last year of high school. She had endless reserves of energy, constantly caring for those close to her and still finding time to make her art and work a full-time job. My brother inherited my father's work ethic and my mother's heart, working 50-plus hours a week building and still managing to be one of the most loving people I knew. Just thinking about their lifestyle used to make me tired.

"So Luka was saying we're going up to your folks' today?" Jenna yelled from the kitchen over the sound of pots and pans banging.

"Yeah, I haven't seen them for months."

"Well, I'm going to make us a stir-fry and then we'll hit the road."

"You're the best."

"I know."

* * *

I remember letting out a sigh of relief once we were away from that city of deferred dreams and communal nightmares. The countryside washed over the car. Jenna drove and told stories about the bizarre scenarios she had to deal with at her job as a nurse.

"I mean, you have a bottle stuck in your asshole, there is no excuse you can make."

"That happens often?"

"Oh, all the time."

We listened to The Pogues, yelling along in shitty Irish

accents. In a small town we bought cheese, sat on the bonnet of the car and ate in the sun. Luka threw a stick for Mr Jenkins, trying to distract him from attacking people.

"Did anyone tell them we were coming?" Jenna asked.

"Not me."

"Nope."

"Should we call them?"

"There's no phone reception for ages. Let's just surprise them."

And so we drove, down through valleys of violent green, along gravel roads that led to hilltops where the landscape rose and fell like waves. The countryside was a guttural scream compared to the restrained madness of the city. Just before we reached my parents' house, the car climbed a steep hill. At the top there was cell phone reception. I checked my phone, expecting a missed call or at least a text from you, but there was nothing.

45 HAMISH

44 ZLATA

WHEN WE PULLED into my parents' place, it was
getting dark. The house sat perched on the edge
of a hill that fell away into a valley, a fast-moving river
slicing through the base. Lights burned in the windows.
Someone peered out at us as we approached, then the door
flew open.

"Oh my god, it's my beautiful children and their beautiful animal," my mother cried, grabbing each of us in turn
and covering us with kisses. She picked up Mr Jenkins,
giving him a friendly shake. "Who's getting fat, hmmm?"
she said, carrying him inside.

We followed her down the short hallway to the open-
plan living room with a messy kitchen in one corner. The
entire interior of the house was made of polished wood.
Rugs, battered couches and armchairs filled the lounge. At
the back of the room were two staircases, one leading up to
my parents' bedroom and the other down to the toilet and
spare rooms. My father sat in an armchair reading, with a

flat-faced cat on his belly. He looked noticeably older than when I had last seen him. What hair he had left was white as paper, his face slack and weathered, but his eyes still burned with the fire I remembered from my childhood. My mother, in contrast, looked relatively unchanged by the passing years. She had gained some weight and moved a little slower, but this suited her disposition.

"Hello! I'd get up but I don't want to disturb ugly here," he said, smiling. I walked over and kissed him on the cheek.

"Good to see you, Dad."

"You too, darling."

"Now if I put this dog down is he going to annoy my animals?" my mother asked.

"Most probably," said Jenna. "He's a real jerk."

"Here, pass him to me, Mum. I'll put him in the spare room for a bit," my brother said.

I stood at the large window that took up most of the back wall. Looking out over the valley, I could see a few lights burning among the trees like fallen stars.

* * *

Later, me and Mum stood in the kitchen. She baked while I drank beer.

"So tell me more about this record deal?" she said, whisking a bowl of cake mix.

"It's nothing definite. But they seem interested."

"And where's Hamish? I thought you would have brought him up."

I finished my beer and went to the fridge for another. "We had a fight."

My mother hugged me, getting cake all over my hoodie. "Was it serious?"

"I think maybe I'm being an idiot, but I don't know. He's so wonderful most of the time. How do you tell?"

"I guess you just decide what you can put up with."

"He has a violent streak."

My mother put the bowl down and looked at me.

"Not towards me."

"Oh, thank god."

"He would never hit me, but then I tolerate him hitting other people all the time. And he sells drugs."

"You know I used to sell drugs."

"Yeah, but it's different. I mean, coke is so fucked."

"Heroin has ruined a couple of lives too. Look, I'm not saying stay with him. Just do what you think is best. Don't make decisions based on what society or Hayley thinks."

I laugh. Hayley is the only person aside from Charlie my mother has ever disapproved of.

"Either way, I feel like I could be making a terrible mistake."

"It's hard for me to say, honey, I've never met the guy."

"I just don't want to be a cliché, you know, attracted to the bad boy kind of thing."

"Don't worry, it's not in your genes," my mother said, pointing the wooden spoon at my father, who was rubbing his face on the belly of the cat. We both laughed.

* * *

The next morning I woke up early. There were no curtains in my room and the sun was staring straight at me. I got up, showered and ate some leftover cake, then took Mr Jenkins for a walk up the hill. I was telling myself I just wanted to give the dog some exercise, but of course it was to check my phone. Just as I reached the summit it beeped. I felt my heart jump, but it was just a text from Hayley: "What happened to dinner last night?"

43 HAMISH

42 ZLATA

AT THE BEACH, waves crashed onto the black sands. On either side of us, tall cliffs loomed up, blocking out the cancerous sun. Behind our backs the forest sat watching. I found myself wondering what you would make of this place. Maybe your anger was bred from our environment. After the art show we could leave, I thought, go somewhere different, at least for a time. But even the most vivid dreams dissipate in the daylight.

My brother took off his T-shirt and picked up Mr Jenkins, screaming at the top of his lungs as he ran into the surf. They were swallowed whole by a wave. Luka dived beneath it while the dog was picked up and dumped onto the sand. The animal got up and looked around, confused, before shaking himself off and trotting back to where me and Jenna were sitting.

"I hope he's careful out there," she said, watching my brother among the waves.

"Don't worry, he's a strong swimmer."

Jenna got some sandwiches out of her backpack. "Okay, so there's hummus, tomato and fake bacon, or cucumber, cheese and marmite."

"I'm not hungry, thanks."

"You should have some before they get sand in them."

"No, thanks."

Jenna began eating.

"I heard you're going out with a drug dealer," she said, between bites. "Or is that a bad thing to say?"

I smiled. "No, it's okay. Yeah, he is, among other things."

"Is it exciting?"

"What?"

"Going out with a criminal."

I laughed and gave Jenna a hug.

"You're so cute sometimes. No, it's not exciting. In fact, it kind of sucks."

"Oh dear."

"It's okay, something will happen."

My brother came running back up the beach.

"Fuck, it's cold. Where's the towel?"

* * *

That night we all ate around the table.

"So how is old Grey Lynn?" my mother asked.

"Same but worse," I replied.

"It can't be that bad if you stay there," Dad said.

"Well, you know, my friends all live there."

"That's right, honey, you stay if you want. It's good for your music."

"There's more to life than music," Dad said.

"Oh Chris, don't start," Mum said, refilling her glass of wine. "She's doing well."

"Yes, but you of all people know how hard it is to support yourself off music."

"And you of all people know how chasing after money leaves you empty and ..."

"Okay, okay, okay," Luka said, putting his hands in the air. "I think we've all heard this argument a million times before."

Both my parents laughed.

"You should think of moving out where we are," said Jenna. "I know it's not cool, but it's cheaper and there's lots of good shops."

"Yeah, maybe." The thought of living in Howick made me feel like killing myself.

My brother laughed. "She's late all the time even when she only has to walk ten minutes."

"You okay?" my father asked me. "You're very quiet."

"Yeah, just tired."

"Are you still taking your pills?"

I felt myself tense, and nodded.

I didn't mention you. It would have upset him. He had moved to Grey Lynn with my mother at the beginning of the '80s. She was pregnant with me and it was the only suburb they could afford to buy into.

"You can see why they call it Grey Lynn," he used to say, pointing to the streets lined with dead trees and broken-down cars. He was from a middle-class family that liked to give the impression they were rich. They scraped together enough to send my father to a private school. Their money and expectations weighed heavy on him.

Grey Lynn's population of Polynesian families, artists and the working class were as foreign to him as my mother's life of political activism, drugs and music. So while my mother became a fixture within the community, organising rallies, playing shows and selling food at the local markets, my father worked tirelessly on building up his accounting business. Five years ago he sold it, along with their house on Prime Road, and moved here. They weren't rich, but with a little luck they wouldn't have to work again. It was confusing enough to him that I would stay there and spend hundreds of dollars a month on rent for substandard housing, let alone that I would start a relationship with someone like you.

41 HAMISH

40 ZLATA

THE NEXT DAY we left late, carrying our bags and hangovers.

"Make sure you come back soon," my mother said, hugging me tightly.

"I will. I love you so much."

"Awww, me too, honey."

* * *

The drive back was more subdued than the trip up. Even Mr Jenkins was quiet. At the top of the hill my phone beeped twice, but it was just Hayley asking where I was, and my friend Jess saying we should get dinner after work tomorrow. I fell in and out of sleep most of the way home. We stopped in a small town an hour out of Auckland and ate hot chips on a park bench by a river. No one said much. I threw some chips into the muddy water and watched the ducks scramble for them. The countryside was growing old.

"We're here," my brother said, shaking me softly. I looked up and saw the flat standing in the dark. My heart sank a little.

"You can come stay with us," he said, and I realised I still hadn't told them what was going on.

"No, it's okay. Thanks, though."

We all got out and I hugged them both.

"That was fun. Let's do it again soon," said Jenna.

"Yeah, for sure."

"Let me know when you have another show," Luka said, handing me my bag.

I watched them drive away to a life that seemed more real than my own. Inside, the house was dark. Opening the bedroom door slowly, I saw our room was empty. I dropped my things and went to the bottle shop.

* * *

You didn't come home that night. The next morning I was almost an hour late to work. I had drunk half a bottle of vodka waiting for you and passed out, still dressed. It was raining and the bus stank of wet clothes. I leaned my head on the seat in front of me and turned up the music on my phone.

"Look who's here," Amber said when I walked in. I felt like screaming, but barely had the energy to speak. I looked at her and felt a brief empathy for your violent outbursts. She was what unimaginative people would call attractive, but her pretty face belied a deep stupidity. Her desk was covered in positive affirmations that made me feel embarrassed for her. I caught sight of myself in the blank monitor as I fell into my chair. I looked awful. My hair was a mess, my eyes sat on top of two heavy bags, my face blotchy and swollen. I turned on the computer and logged in.

There was an email from Louisa.

Hey hey,

Want to do a show with us at Whammy next month?

Free beer and we'll split the door.

Let me know asap,

Love Lou

Amber walked over. "We have to get this stuff logged before lunch," she said, handing me some receipts.

I went to the toilet and threw up.

* * *

Me and Jess had been lovers for a brief stint. In simpler times, before my breakdown. I called things off to be with Charlie, something I deeply regretted on the rare occasion I allowed myself to think about it. After not speaking for a year we became close friends. I arrived late and saw her at the bar hunched over a huge can of Asahi. I walked up behind her and squeezed her sides. She spun around and for a second I thought she was going to hit me.

"Jesus, babe, you gave me a fright."

"Sorry." I took a seat next to her. She was voluptuous with an ass that mocked gravity, her top lip curled up to give her mouth a constant pout. Everything about her screamed *sex* except her eyes, which flashed innocence if you watched closely. I ordered a can of beer for myself.

"God, I need this," I said.

"You look like shit."

"I know."

"The musician lifestyle getting to you?"

"More my love life." The beer came and I took a long drink, feeling my body relax as the alcohol entered my system.

"Who are you seeing now?"

"This guy Hamish."

"Not Rapley's friend?"

"Yeah, you know them?"

"Yeah, we used to get wasted together. They were pretty wild. Rapley's cool. Don't really know Hamish that well."

"They're still pretty wild."

Jess laughed. "Maybe to you, babe. Anyway, what are we going to eat?"

* * *

After dinner we walked across Hopetoun Bridge. It was dark and drizzling. I looked back towards the city. From this distance you could mistake it for a place where things actually happened. I watched the cars crawling over the harbour bridge. Jess grew up on the other side, on the shore, in a suburb she escaped as soon as possible. People from places that are impossible to love seem to avoid abandonment issues.

"You should come for dinner next week," Jess said.

"Yeah, sounds good."

"Maybe bring your man if things work out."

"Maybe."

"Cheer up. You're about to make an album."

"I know. Sorry."

"You should be. I hardly ever see you, and when I do you're all mopey."

We reached the corner of Ponsonby Road and Williamson Ave.

"I hope it works out," Jess said, hugging me. "And if it doesn't, you can come and stay with me."

"Thanks," I said, still holding onto her. Cars sped past, their tyres hissing at us.

* * *

When I got home, you were asleep in bed. I stood there staring at you. And then took off my clothes and stood in the shower until the hot water ran out.

39 HAMISH

I WAKE TO the sound of Zlata playing the guitar. I feel like shit: mouth dry, heart racing. I sit up, squinting into the dark.

"Hey," Zlata says. It's not her usual voice. She's sitting on the floor with her back to me.

"What time is it?"

"Nine."

With great effort I crawl out of bed and walk over. I reach out to touch her. She hits my hand away.

"Don't."

I'm standing there looking down at her, feeling like my blood's been replaced with petrol. She stops playing, turns and stares up at me, her eyes so angry.

"I'm sorry." My voice is weak.

"You know, after you hit Jacob at Hayley's party I decided to give you another chance. And now you've fucked that up." She starts playing again, strumming the same chords over and over. "I love you, Hamish, but if I stay and you do something like this again it'll kill me."

I watch her small hand moving around the neck of the guitar.

"Why didn't you call?"

"I was ashamed." I sit on the edge of the bed. "I was angry at myself, but I took it out on you." She stares at me again.

"Where have you been?" she asks.

"Smoking shit with Skam and that."

"The whole time?"

"Pretty much."

She shakes her head.

"I thought you didn't do that."

"I haven't for years. I don't know."

We're both quiet now.

"I'm going to go to sleep," she says. "I have to go to work tomorrow."

I try to touch her as she walks past. This time she softly pushes my hand away.

"Not yet."

* * *

The bed and my stomach are empty when I wake up. Apart from a jar of mustard, there isn't any food in the house. I walk up to the café where Nicholas works. It's full of rich people drinking coffee, standing around looking like fuckwits. I push past to the counter, where I get Nicholas's attention.

"How you doing, brother?" Even at work he's dressed like a miniature male model.

"Hey, bro."

"You want some food?"

"Yeah, I'm starving."

"Take a seat, I'll bring it out."

I sit by the window. I feel fucking awful. The last few days are a blur. We were holed up in one of Skam's mate's houses most of the time. That place was so depressing. There was a fight at one point, I remember that. Nicholas brings over a plate of eggs benedict with bacon, and sits down opposite.

"What's been happening?" he asks.

"I fucked up."

"Really? That's not like you." He smiles.

"I think I've ruined shit with Zlata."

"That's a shame, man."

"I feel like I'm broken or something."

"That's bullshit. If you want to make things work you can."

"Yeah."

"Like Rapley keeps saying, quit dealing, concentrate on your art."

"True."

"You're talented, stop wasting time."

"Thanks, man."

"Look I got to get back, brother. You'll be okay," he says, giving me a hug.

"Yep," I say, squeezing him back.

* * *

It's midnight, I'm in the studio. I can't bring myself to paint. I'm listening to Zlata's demos and pouring a bottle of whisky down my throat.

I hear footsteps on the stairs and the door bursts open.

"Good morning, Captain!" Jamil yells, walking in followed by Skam.

"'Sup?" Jamil sits down while Skam stands by the door.

"Oh, you know, this and that." I take out a plastic bag full of powder, throw it on the table.

"This is it."

"So you're really going to quit?"

"Yep."

"That's a shame. Now I'm going to have to deal with dodgy cunts again."

"I'm sure you'll manage."

"Yeah, I suppose." He takes the bag and looks at it. "Oh well," he says, pulling out a wad of cash and chucking it on the table, "now you can buy a nice suit or a shit car with all of that."

* * *

I get home. Zlata's asleep. I want to talk to her but it's probably not a good idea. In the living room, Jean and Bella are still up, watching a zombie show.

"Hey," I say, falling onto the couch.

"He's back," says Bella.

"Do you like my new outfit?" asks Jean, standing up. She's wearing a light-blue track suit with white stripes.

"It makes you look like a giant baby."

"Thanks," she smiles.

"Things okay with you and Zlata?" Bella asks.

"Yeah."

"'Cos she seemed pretty upset."

On the TV, two zombies are ripping a man in half.

"It's hard living with people sometimes," says Jean. "I was living with my ex and she used to eat everything, like everything. The onions, the flour, everything."

"What?" I say.

"Don't worry. So you like the track suit?"

* * *

I wake up early the next morning. Zlata's gone again. I get down a Nike shoebox from the top of my wardrobe, empty a pile of cash onto the bed. I add the money Jamil gave me and count it. In total I got almost $5000. I'm hoping it'll last till after the show. I put the box back on top of the wardrobe and lie down again. I feel better for the first time in days. Maybe things will be okay.

38 ZLATA

WHEN I LEFT work that evening you were standing across the road, leaning up against the wall, your cap low, covering your sad brown eyes. When you saw me, you waved and ran into traffic, dancing between the oncoming cars.

"Hey," you said, out of breath.

"Hello." I was swaying back and forth, trying to distract myself from the exhaustion filling every inch of me.

"Wanna get dinner?" You somehow managed to look up at me, even though you were a head taller.

"Okay, should we go to the food court?"

"I've got us a table at that Japanese place in Ponsonby."

"The fancy pants one?"

"Yeah."

"Oh, okay then." You smiled and took my hand.

"Let's get a cab."

"What's going on?" I asked, dropping your hand. "You're not going to tell me you've got AIDS or something are you?"

"What? No."

* * *

We were the only poor people in the restaurant. You got so nervous around displays of wealth so I knew it was a big deal that you took me there. We sat at a low square table while waiters, dressed like Japanese people in movies, hurried around us. You ordered sake while I scanned the menu. The entrées cost more than I would usually spend on a main. I hoped you were paying.

We drank the sake quickly and you ordered another. The warm liquor dissolved some of the anger I was carrying in my gut.

"There's some shit I need to say," you said, leaning forward on your elbows, your eyes just visible beneath the brim of your cap. I watched you trying to drag out the words.

"Ummm," you paused and looked at me. I should have smiled, but I refused to make this easy for you.

"I'm really fucking sorry." You shook your head. "Meeting you has made me feel shit. It's scary."

You let out a breath like you were in pain.

"Like, growing up it was cool to be numb, you know, start fucking young as possible, take drugs, drink till you go crazy, punch people for no reason, do everything and act like it was nothing." You stopped and looked up at me. "And now all of a sudden I feel all this shit and ... I don't know."

You put your head down again. I reached across the table and took your hand.

"And I quit."

You scratched your face and sighed again.

"Quit what?"

"Dealing."

"Really?"

"Yeah, I got some money, till the show, and then I guess I'll get a job. I don't want to lose you."

You stopped and screwed up your face.

"It would be so shit." You leaned back in your chair.

I said yes.

I said I love you.

I said I forgive you.

When what I meant was 'I am so tired'.

* * *

We walked home through Cox's Creek. The park, which I wouldn't have set foot in alone at night, seemed to welcome us. The trees shielded the lights from nearby houses. We stood in the middle of the field and kissed, high on the synthetic happiness of reconciliation. We held hands and walked by the creek filled with sewage and the rotting corpses of dead pets. People swam there in the '50s. They will say similarly absurd things about us one day.

37 HAMISH

I'M FEELING REALLY nervous. I haven't been up to the studio for days. I spent the whole weekend ignoring Rapley's texts. I'm standing outside the red door, the street's busy. I'm too ashamed to go up.

"Hamish!" Luke yells, waving from a bench packed with teenagers. I walk over and shove them.

"Move over, dicks." One of the kids gets up and I take his seat.

"Heard you were on the pipe this weekend," Luke says, with a cheeky grin.

"Whatever." I give him a hug.

"Heard there was a fight."

"Nah."

"You got any buds?" asks the kid with the freckles.

"Yeah, upstairs."

Rapley's painting with his back to the door. He's been busy since I was last up here. The studio's even more messy than usual.

"Hey," I say.

"Yo," he replies without turning round. I go to my desk, pull out a bag of weed and throw it to Luke.

"Can I have all of it?" he asks, surprised.

"Yeah, take it, man," The kids crowd around Luke, buzzing out about the weed.

"Fucking sweet," one of them says.

"So you going to do some art, Santa Claus?" Rapley asks. "You know, for your first show?"

"Yeah man, Zlata went AWOL and ..."

"I don't care bro, we need to get this shit happening."

"True."

"The gallery wants to come get some photos next week and they lined up some press."

"Yous going to be on TV?" Freckle Face asks.

"*Police Ten 7*," says Luke.

The kids all crack up.

"All right, fuck off for a bit," says Rapley.

"Ahhh but ..."

"Go smoke in the park."

The kids shuffle out. I walk over to Rapley.

"We good?" I ask. He shrugs.

"I quit, man."

"Dealing?"

"Yeah."

"That's cool."

I wait for him to say something else. When it's obvious he's not going to I get out my paints and start working on a canvas.

* * *

"Those DMT dudes are in the park," Luke says, running up the stairs followed by his little gang, all of them stinking of weed.

Out the window there's four or five guys looking up at us. I recognise one of the dudes we gave a hiding to.

"They say they want yous to come down."

"Did they try and fuck with you?" I ask Luke.

"Nah."

"Fuck them," Rapley's giving them the fingers.

"I got this if you need it," Luke pulls out the hunting knife.

"The fuck, Luke?!" I yell, "I told you to get rid of that."

"I know, but …"

"Give it to me." I snatch it. "You want someone to stab you?"

The kids all look at their shoes. I throw the knife on top of one of the cupboards just as a rock hits the window.

Me and Luke peer out.

"Persistent, aren't they?

I write 'toys' on a piece of paper, tape it to the glass. Below they all start yelling and flapping their arms around.

"Look at this," I say to Rapley. He leans over and starts laughing.

"Fucking eggs."

* * *

I'm listening to Townes Van Zandt, walking down Crummer Road. When my father fucked off, the only things he left behind were the shell of my mother and a pile of country and folk records. I got Rapley into it — we used to smoke weed and listen to them at my place when my mum was working at the TAB. It's kind of cool now, but when we were young, we got given so much shit for being into that stuff. But everything changes, right? Look at this place. I remember being so scared walking down this street at night. Back before I learnt to fight, we used to get jumped and chased every other time we went outside. Now the only thing to worry about round here's the rent.

When I get home Zlata's asleep. I take off my clothes and fall into bed with her.

"Hey," I whisper. She's quietly snoring, her back to me. I pull her close. "I love coming home to you," I whisper. She keeps snoring. I kiss the back of her neck. "You make me so happy."

36 ZLATA

EVERYONE WAS AT Louisa's wearing their shittiest
clothes; Sam, Lou, Luke and Freckles. Sam was
mixing up flour and water in two 40-litre buckets with a
drum stick. Luke passed round a joint and talked endlessly
about Rapley and you, gesturing wildly with his long thin
arms.

"And then they were like, 'Tell them to come outside,
we'll fuck them up'. And Rapley, he didn't even care, he was
like, fuck it." He took another toke. "He didn't give a fuck."

"Hey, Luke," Sam said.

"Yeah?"

"Shut up."

The kid looked at the ground and took another drag.

"So we got 200 posters," said Louisa. "We should split
into two groups. One half do Ponsonby, Grey Lynn and
Sandringham. The other hit up K Road, Grafton and
Symonds Street."

"I bags Zlata," said Sam.

"Okay, I'll go with Freckles."

"You better do some work," Sam said, pointing the drum stick at Luke.

* * *

We took turns carrying the bucket, the paste spilling onto the crumbling footpath.

Symonds Street was once a creative hub, before becoming a row of fast food franchises and digital printers. (Even cancer is a form of progress.)

Me and Luke held the posters in place while Sam brushed the thick white paste over them, standing on her tiptoes to reach the top. Rapley had made the poster in exchange for beer; it featured two fat babies screaming the band names and venue details.

"Hold it straight," Sam kept yelling. "Do you want people to think this is some kind of Mickey Mouse operation?"

"My arms are sore," Luke whined.

"Stop wanking so much then."

A cop car rolled past slowly and we stopped and stood around looking guilty. The car kept driving.

"Fucking pigs," said Luke.

"I bet you've never even been in the cells," Sam said, flicking him with paste.

"Fuck off."

"I'm excited to do this show," I said. "I think it'll sell out."

"Good, I'm so broke."

"Get a job," said Luke.

"You can talk, you live at home."

"I'm only 17."

"Exactly. Anyway, there's no fucking jobs. Where do you think you live, Melbourne?"

"I thought you were on the benefit?" I said to Sam.

"Got kicked off, fuck them. Just need to tour again."

"You should get our rap group to open for you on tour," Luke said.

"You have a rap group?" I asked.

Sam shook her head. "Now you've done it."

"Yeah ... do you want to hear a verse?"

"No!" Sam yelled.

"But ..."

"If you rhyme two words together, I'm gonna tip this whole bucket of paste over your head."

* * *

Back at Louisa's everyone was talking fast, high off the night. The freckle-faced kid had stolen a bottle of whisky on his travels. He pulled it out of his backpack and placed it proudly on the coffee table.

"Isn't that cute," said Louisa, rubbing his thin red hair. "I'll get some glasses." Freckles stood there, beaming.

Sam put on some screamy punk group and fell onto the couch next to me.

"So, things good with you and Hammy again?"

"Yeah, the last week has been wonderful."

"You're like me with my antidepressants — on, off, on, off." We both laughed.

"He actually opened up."

"Really? Shit, he must like you. Did he do that thing where he looks like he's having a migraine."

"YES!"

We both laughed.

Everyone drank and talked about plans for the future. Later the kids passed out and me and Sam danced to The Smiths. Though work was only five hours away, I felt free.

* * *

That morning a sadness blanketed the streets, thin like frost. You could scrape it off with your hand. But it wasn't cold, it felt like nothing. Condensation from a million dreams. Was it any wonder that everyone was drunk and high all the time? Spectators of their own lives. What control can you have when you must choose between doing what you love and surviving? Either way you starved.

I left work at lunchtime, caught the bus to Ponsonby Road and started walking down Williamson. In the distance I saw a white Honda Civic driving erratically. Just before it reached me, the car mounted the footpath with a screeching of brakes.

"Fuck!" I screamed, leaping back as the car came within inches of hitting me. The doors flew open and Sam, Luke and Louisa fell out, laughing hysterically.

"Oh my god, you should have seen your face," Sam gasped.

"Oh look, she's all put out," said Lou, coming up and giving me a hug.

"I'm way too hungover for these shenanigans," I said, giving in and laughing.

"Come with us, we're going to the chemist to get some medicine."

"Whose car is this?"

"It's my mum's, she's in the hospital again," said Luke.

"And you're letting Sam drive it?"

"Everyone else is drunk."

I got in the back seat and my phone beeped. It was a text from Sam. "I'm drunk too. Shhhh."

I did my seatbelt up.

* * *

We stopped out front of the chemist on Surrey Crescent.

"Who's going in?" Sam asked.

Everyone looked at me. "What's going on?"

"We need some cough medicine."

"Who's sick?"

Everyone laughed.

"No, it's got morphine in it. We have headaches and boring lives," said Louisa.

"Why can't someone else go in?"

"Luke's too young, I go in all the time and Sam looks like someone who would get high on cough medicine."

"You saying I look like a junkie?"

"No, your face is too fat," said Luke. This was answered with a whack on the head.

"I don't know ..." I said.

"It's easy."

"Come on, my brain has AIDS," Sam pleads.

I got out of the car and walked in. A small Indian woman with a calm smile walked over to me. I told her I was after some cough medicine and she led me to the shelf. I saw the bottle straight away and picked it up.

"This is cheaper and you get more," the woman says, holding up a bottle of Robitussin.

"No thanks, I want this."

"Why?"

"Because ... I don't know."

"I'm not going to sell it to you."

I stood there trying to think of something to say.

"I don't care," I said, and slammed the bottle back on the shelf.

* * *

"I don't care?"

Back in the car everyone was laughing at me again. "I don't care," Sam kept repeating.

"Sam, give me your backpack," says Luke.

"Why?"

"I'll get the shit. You come in and distract her."

Sam and Luke walked into the store.

"You coming to the Coromandel?" Lou asked.

"Yeah I think so."

"You should. It's always heaps of fun when we go. We should bring guitars and work on songs."

"That would be great. I'd love to write with you guys."

Luke walked quickly out of the chemist and jumped in the car.

"We need to go," he said.

"Sam has the keys."

"What the fuck is she doing?"

Luke sank down into the seat, then Sam came out smiling. She walked slowly towards the car.

"Did you get the shit?" she asked, starting the engine.

"I got all of it," Luke opened the bag. It was filled with bottles of cough medicine.

"I LOVE TUESDAY!" Sam yelled, stomping on the accelerator and stalling the car.

35 HAMISH

ME AND RAPLEY are painting, listening to
Ghostface.

We've been in the studio for hours, smoking weed and
working. My phone beeps.

"Zlata's at Louisa's. You want to head down?"

"Yeah, let's do it," Rapley says. "I'm getting cabin fever."

I start packing my shit up.

"Hey," Rapley says, shoving some cans into his
backpack, "I'm glad you quit. I feel like we could get
something happening with all this."

I nod my head. I don't know what to say.

"Come here," he says, hugging me.

* * *

Out on K Road the street's dead.

"They drinking?" he asks.

"I'm off the booze for a bit."

"Whatever."

Up ahead someone runs towards us. A tall guy, clean-cut, with nice clothes. He sprints past, looking real scared.

"What the fuck?" says Rapley.

Skam and Jamil come flying around the corner. They see us and slow down to a casual walk. "Fellas," says Jamil, out of breath.

"Who was that?"

"Who was who?"

"The preppy dude you were chasing."

Jamil shrugs his shoulders, Skam acts like he hasn't heard me.

"What are yous up to?" Jamil asks.

"Going to Louisa's."

Jamil looks bummed. "She banned me from her place."

"Is there anywhere you're not banned from?"

"Owl bar."

"That must be fun."

"Let's go find that American cunt," Jamil says, and they take off down the road.

* * *

Everyone's crowded around a giant TV. Louisa's driving in circles. Luke veers off the road, wide-eyed and laughing. The Nintendo console is older than he is.

"Look who's here," says Zlata, stumbling towards me. She puts her arms round my waist and kisses me. She tastes like Christmas cake icing.

"What you guys been drinking?"

Sam reaches into her backpack and throws a bottle at me.

"Cough medicine?" I pass it to Rapley.

"You got something to chase this?" Rapley asks.

"There's Fanta in the kitchen," Louisa says, staring at the screen.

"Go halves?" Rapley says.

"Fuck it, why not?" In the kitchen we pour the thick light brown liquid into two cups.

"I hate this shit," I say, holding it up to the light.

"Better than nothing." Rapley knocks his back and takes a swig of Fanta. "Fuck," he mutters.

The syrup burns my throat. I reach for the soft drink but Rapley snatches it away, the dick. My eyes are watering, I can't see shit. I stumble to the sink, drink water out of the tap.

"Thanks, asshole," I say, as he laughs at me.

34 ZLATA

IT WAS GETTING colder, the nights longer. We had spent the last few weeks in our own worlds and tonight we would emerge for a few glorious hours. I had sound-checked and was back at mine getting ready. I tried on my blue dress. It looked good but I was worried I wouldn't be able to move around on stage. Someone knocked at the door.

"What're you doing in there?" Hayley yelled from behind the door.

"Help me decide what to wear."

She walked in and sat on the bed looking immaculate, as always.

"Well don't wear that — it makes you look short and like you like cakes."

"I am short and I love cakes."

"Yes, but you want to maintain some degree of class." She got up and riffled through my closet.

"What about this thing?" She held up a green dress I got in Thailand.

"No, too short."

"What's wrong with short?"

"I don't want people to see my ass when I'm adjusting my pedals."

"This one?"

"No, I think I'm just going to wear jeans and a T-shirt."

Hayley dropped the dress she was holding and put her hands on her hips.

"God, you give up so easy."

"It's a show, I need to be comfortable."

"Okay, fine, look like shit."

* * *

I was nervous about the new songs. Would they dance once I let them go? We were in a taxi. I leaned my face on the cold glass, watching the streets. I felt like walking but Hayley had ridiculous shoes on. I loved the neighbourhood at this time on weekends. It was empty, everyone at home getting ready, the air charged with excitement. We thought every weekend would be different — gamblers, believing this time we would beat the house. The next morning we would wake up broke and sick, swearing never again. But by afternoon we were feeling lucky and it would begin all over.

St Kevin's Arcade was already crowded with people drinking on the steps when we arrived. I saw your young friends and exchanged waves as I walked into the venue. I'm not one of those people that longs to be a teenager again. Those with anxiety learn how to live later in life. But seeing their young faces laughing on concrete stairs in the middle of winter, I missed that bedlam. You could be at a party with a bottle of cheap wine and your friends, or watch movies in bed all weekend — either way it was a celebration.

The venue smelt like stale beer and piss. The pipes in the roof leaked. You just hoped you were drunk enough not to care. I recognised the girl on the door from past shows. I had made a fool of myself hitting on her last year after a gig. She was too beautiful, like some kind of genetic joke.

"Hey," I said, walking quickly past. She said something I didn't hear. Joe was at the bar, looking tired.

"Hello, Joseph," I said, pulling up a stool.

"Zlata. Want a beer?"

"Yes, I do."

The place was still pretty empty. No one ventured out in this town until they were drunk enough to brave the claustrophobia. Joe placed a beer in front of me.

"I heard you're doing new stuff tonight."

"Yeah, mostly."

"I love that one song that's been on the radio a bit. The one about your work."

I laughed. "You know she's a real person?"

"No?!"

"Yeah." A few more people bustled in. I scanned the room again but saw no sign of Sam or Louisa.

"It fucking stinks down here," said Hayley, hobbling over.

"Where did you go?"

"Christina had to get cash out."

"I got kicked out of here last time," said Christina.

"I don't want to touch anything," said Hayley, holding her hands in the air.

"Don't act so precious. You work in a fucking strip club," snapped Christina.

"Where's Alice tonight?" I asked.

"With the little ones," Hayley said, and then turned back to Christina. "At least I have a job."

"Oh, and what a fucking achievement ..."

I walked over to the stage and pretended to be setting up gear.

* * *

By 11:30 there was no sign of Fuck Yous and the place was starting to fill up.

I was sitting in between Christina and Hayley, trying to get them to stop fighting.

"Where's Hamish?" Christina asked.

"He's not selling drugs any more," Hayley said.

"Fuck you."

Hayley got up. "Look after my stuff," she said to me and walked off.

"You know, this show is quite stressful for me as it is," I said.

Christina grabbed my arm. "I know, I'm sorry, we should be kept apart." She reached into her pocket and held her hand out to me.

"What is it?"

"OxyContin."

"I'm okay."

"Just take it. It'll make you relax. I feel bad now."

I put out my hand and she dropped the green pill into it. I washed it down with beer.

"How have you been?" I asked.

"Good. I'm going to go back to uni."

"That's great. What will you study?"

"Politics. I have half a degree already."

* * *

We danced around the reason she had left uni in the first place. I wondered if you had sold her the drugs that led to her addiction. And if so, were you to blame? I looked at her: she was still young but had a brittleness of someone much older. Hayley always spoke of Christina's addiction as if it were some flaw in her character, but it could happen to anyone. Before she started getting high, Christina barely drank. She was top of her class at school. I think that's where a lot of Hayley's resentment came from. Christina was the star pupil while Hayley was the pretty dyslexic who dated charmless rich boys.

"What's up?" Christina asked me. "Why are you staring at me like that?"

"Sorry, just thinking."

The support band was starting.

"Let's go watch," I said.

33 HAMISH

IT TAKES FUCKING forever to get in 'cos Rapley's flirting with the girl on the door. I can hear Zlata talking to the crowd. When we finally make it inside, the place is packed.

"This is the first time I've done most of these songs, so be kind."

People cheer. I push up the front.

"Okay, I'm just going to make sure my bass player and drummer are ready and then we'll make some music."

She turns and starts fucking with the drum machine. The music kicks in and Zlata grabs the microphone and starts to sing.

The song's fast and crazy in the verses but the chorus drops back, just Zlata and the drums. The crowd's dancing, the room's hot. I can hardly breathe. The song finishes and we all cheer.

"Awww, thank you. That song's about my boyfriend. Is he here?"

I'm trying to duck behind the person in front of me but Rapley picks me up under my arms.

"Here he is!" he yells.

"Hello, baby. Everyone look at my boyfriend."

I cover my face with my hands while they all laugh.

"This song is about my job, it's called 'I Hope that's Work-Related'."

* * *

Zlata's surrounded by people before she even gets off the stage. She's so pretty, smiling and shaking hands.

Nicholas comes and puts his arm round my shoulder.

"Your girlfriend's really talented," he says.

"I know."

"So are you, man." He's rubbing my back now.

"Have you taken a pill?"

"Yeah," he says, smiling like lunatic, his eyes too big for his sockets. The crowd around Zlata has thinned out.

"I'm going to go and talk to Zlata."

"Okay," he says, following me.

"That was so good," I say, hugging her. She's soaked with sweat.

"You think? Oh god, I'm disgusting and I didn't remember to bring anything to change into."

"This is Nicholas, your number one fan."

He throws his arms around Zlata. "That was absolutely spectacular."

"Thanks," Zlata says, looking at me wide-eyed over his shoulder.

"You're very moist ..."

I slap him across the top of his head.

"Don't say 'moist' to my girlfriend."

"She is though, feel her."

"Sorry, he's high."

* * *

Sam and Louisa turn up twenty minutes after they're supposed to be on stage. Sam's so drunk she can barely walk.

"Okay, we're here!" she screams, falling into a group of awkward dudes with funny caps on. They all try to step away from her.

"Who pushed me?" she yells.

Louisa gets on stage and start tuning.

"Check," Louisa says into the mic. "Sam, come set up your shit."

"I'm getting a beer!" she screams.

"There's beers here."

"FUCK, YEAH!" She punches her fist in the air and staggers towards the stage.

"I'm so excited for your exhibition," says Nicholas, rubbing my back again. "You know, I really look up to you guys."

"Thanks," I say, wishing he'd stop touching me.

* * *

Louisa's standing on stage looking impatient while Sam fucks around with her drums. After five minutes she's finally ready.

"Okay, this song is called 'I Hate your Band but I Let you Open for us Because your Fans go to Art School and have Disposable Incomes'," Lou yells. Sam counts in and, for a pisshead, she does a decent job of drumming. The songs are fast and catchy. They smash out 15 or 16 in about half an hour. Sam's drumming starts turning to shit by the halfway mark. She keeps dropping her sticks. I can tell Louisa's getting pissed off.

"Okay, that's the last song."

"Nah, we got two more," yells Sam. Louisa ignores her and starts packing up her shit. The crowd doesn't know whether to stick around or go smoke. Sam and Louisa start arguing at the back of the stage. Sam kicks over the snare drum and walks into the crowd.

* * *

I find her outside sitting on the steps, crying.

"Hey, what's wrong?" I ask, sitting next to her.

"Fucking everything."

"That wasn't so bad."

"It sucked, but I don't care about that."

"What's up, then?"

"Fucking Jerry doesn't want to see me any more."

"Who?"

"The American."

"The rollerblader?"

"Oh god, I'm crying about someone who rollerblades," she laughs through her tears. I hug her.

"Why would he not want to see you?"

"'Cos I'm crazy and ugly and my friends are all psychos and keep beating him up."

"Don't say that. You're not ugly."

"I love you."

"I love you too. Come on, everyone's going back to Louisa's. I'll shout us a cab."

32 ZLATA

THE OFFICE WAS stuffy; the walls lined with photos of bands I hated. In one corner a small stereo quietly played glorified elevator music. We sat around a table filled with stale cake and cold coffee. Flies circled the food. No one made any move to shoo them away. In front of me the label rep talked quickly about how much he loved the show. I knew he hadn't been there, his name wasn't crossed off the guest list. He was younger than me, brimming with dishonest enthusiasm. Next to him was an overweight woman wearing too much make-up. She kept adding to the ends of the rep's sentences. They both stopped talking and smiled at me. I had stopped listening long ago and simply smiled back. Eventually theirs began to falter.

"So, what do you think?" the rep asked, sounding unsure of himself for the first time.

"Yeah, I think if I can get a copy of the contract I'll take it to my lawyer." As if I had a lawyer, but the flies were making me feel sick and I wanted to get out of that place.

"Yes, of course." We all stood up and shook hands. The fat woman made a joke about some current news story. I made a noise resembling a laugh and quickly made my way to the elevator.

It was almost rush hour when I got out. I walked home, kicking tennis ball-sized chunks of the footpath onto the road. I'd always dreamed of getting a record deal, but it was hard to imagine anything of beauty coming out of that office. Besides, how could you trust those people? They reminded me of Amber, trying to hide their ignorance behind expensive clothes and pained smiles. But if you peeled back the veneer of control and professionalism they were in the same downward spiral as everyone else.

I moved slowly through the dusk, in no hurry to get anywhere. You were at the studio and Bella and Jean were in Australia. I wouldn't be able to write. I felt sick with confusion. I wanted to ask someone's advice. I knew you would say 'Fuck the label', and of course Hayley would tell me to take the deal. I tried my mum but she didn't answer the landline and there was never any point ringing her cell phone.

* * *

Louisa was on the couch playing her guitar quietly. Timothy lay asleep next to her. The twins played Mario Karts with the sound off.

"It's hard because you're right, they will fuck it up. They sent our single to the radio and then forgot to service the video for two months." Timothy stirred and Louisa stopped playing and stroked his head. "But at the same time, they have a little money and can get you promo."

"I wish I was in a band sometimes."

"You think Sam is any help in situations like this?" We both laughed. "Look, your songs are really good. Either way, it'll work out."

"I just got to find something other than that office job."

"I can imagine, it must be an awful place to work."

Timothy sat up. "Where's Dad?" he asked.

Louisa sighed. "Probably at the pub, honey."

* * *

Walking home, my stomach hurt. Back then I still believed failure to be the worst possible outcome in any given situation. I saw life as a series of puzzles that must be solved correctly in order to succeed. It never occurred to me that any success, no matter how grand, dissipates as soon as it's realised. You're left performing increasingly dangerous feats to keep people's interest. And sooner or later you will slip.

31 HAMISH

WE'RE FOLLOWING NICHOLAS in his new Audi. Every twenty minutes they stop so Sam can piss, buy treats or whatever the fuck she's doing.

"How did he afford that car?" Jess asks.

"He works all the time and sells his art."

"That'll be you soon, Hammy." Zlata turns, grabbing my hand.

"I don't know 'bout that."

"I can't believe they're fucking stopping again," Jess says, whacking the steering wheel so hard me and Zlata both jump. Sam leaps out, runs into the gas station.

"Does she have a bladder infection or something?" Jess asks.

"Nah, it's 'cos she's drinking a litre of coke every ten kilometres."

Sam comes out, shaking up a 1.5 litre bottle of Fanta.

"What's she doing now?"

She undoes the lid and sprays Nicholas's car with the orange liquid.

"Oh, he's not going to like that," Zlata says, shaking her head.

Nicholas gets out and starts yelling at Sam. She stands there drinking what's left of the Fanta and then walks over to our car.

"She better not get any of that shit in here," says Jess.

"Move over." Sam shoves me with a sticky hand.

"Seriously, we're not stopping till Coromandel, okay?" says Jess, speeding out of the car park.

* * *

It's a Thursday, the roads are quiet. Jess drives impatiently behind Nick, pulling out to overtake, then falling back again.

"You'd think he could drive a bit faster with that car," she grumbles to herself.

"There's no hurry," I say.

"I know where we're going," says Sam.

"You do?"

"Yeah."

Jess pulls into the right-hand lane. We speed past, Sam leaning out the window, giving them the fingers and spitting at Nick's car.

"Get the fuck back in the car," Jess yells.

* * *

We come to a long bridge and race across. Beneath us, muddy water makes its way out to the ocean.

"Can we stop in Thames?" Sam asks.

"No, wait until we get to Coromandel," Jess says.

"But I need to piss."

"Hold on."

"I'll piss in your car."

"Do it and see what happens."

Sam starts saying something, then turns and looks out the window. We pass through Thames. Empty shops line the wide streets. A few teenagers wander aimlessly. A skinny dog limps across the road.

"This is the happiest place on earth," Sam sings.

"Don't sing that stupid song," snaps Jess.

* * *

"Are you sure it's left?"

It's almost dark now. We're parked up on the side of some turnoff. Sam keeps saying we need to pull onto this tiny dirt road to get to the house. I look behind us, there's no sign of the Audi.

"I've been there like a hundred times. It's this way."

"Maybe we should wait for the others," Zlata says.

"Fuck, just go, then we can get drunk," Sam says.

Jess shrugs and pulls onto the dirt road. Giant trees whack the side of the car. Every so often lights from a house peer out at us from the bush. This place is real creepy. We start to climb a steep hill; the car is straining. The road's getting worse and worse. By the time we reach the top of the hill, it's like a fucking goat track. Jess pulls the handbrake and turns to face Sam.

"So, I think we can safely say this isn't the way," she mutters.

"I'm sure they said we went through the township," Zlata says.

"Fuck, Sam."

"I'm going to take a piss," she says getting out of the car.

"Let's fucking leave her here," Jess says, blue eyes burning.

* * *

We find Nicholas and the others waiting in town. By the time we reach the house, it's late as fuck. The cars crawl down the long gravel driveway. The headlights shine on the bach, which is covered in red peeling paint. We park, everyone gets out groaning and stretching. Inside it's just two rooms; a lounge and kitchen area, and a bedroom filled with mattresses. Louisa starts opening the windows while Rapley fucks round with the fuse box.

"Have a look out the back," Louisa yells from the bedroom.

We walk round the side of the house, following a sandy path that cuts through some dead-looking trees. After a few minutes we're standing on a beach. I can't see the water but can hear the waves crashing.

"Wow," says Zlata, sitting down in the sand. "What an amazing place."

"Whose is it?" Rapley asks.

"Don't know. Louisa's aunt or cousin or some shit."

We sit listening to the waves. I put my arm around Zlata. Sometimes we are lucky.

"This is boring," Sam says, jumping to her feet.

"Where do you think you're going?" Rapley yells, putting her over his shoulder and running towards the ocean.

"You want to go for a swim?" he says. "Are you sure?"

"No, put me down, you big lummox!" Sam yells, feebly hitting his back.

We follow, pulling off our clothes. Rapley runs into the

ocean, still holding Sam, and dives under. The rest of us follow. The water's fucking freezing.

"Jesus Christ."

I come up and look back towards the shore, where Zlata's sitting on the sand.

"What's wrong?" I call to her.

"Nothing."

"Come in, it's nice."

"I'm okay."

Then Sam leaps on my back, pushing me under.

30 ZLATA

THERE WAS A HOLE in the roof. I lay in bed watching the clouds float past. The day scratched at the doors and windows, waking everyone, and the room filled with groans and coughs. People asking rhetorical questions in strained voices.

"What happened?"

"How much did I drink?"

Sam walked outside and vomited on the front deck.

"Fuck, couldn't you have gone in the bushes?" Jess shouts.

I drank some water and, when that had no effect, a beer. Jess started cooking up beans and onions. Walking up behind her, I hugged her round belly.

"Hello, Jessica."

"Hey, you." I looked over her shoulder, watching her cook. The food smelled so good; despite the urge to be sick I was hungry. Sam came back into the house, wiping her mouth on the back of her hand.

"I feel like dying," she said, throwing herself back onto her bed.

"The little pest overdid it," Jess said, shooting her a look.

I stared out the window. The sun was already spreading itself over the tree-covered hills.

* * *

We spent the day frivolously, lying in the sun, eating and drinking beer. Louisa spoke about quitting music and getting her life together, then twenty minutes later was talking of how amazing the European tour was going to be. Rapley talked of how the neighbourhood had changed. Jess, who had moved to Grey Lynn in the last five years, said we needed to let go of the past, and we all went quiet.

I gorged myself at least three times and drank so much beer I was staggering by the time the shadows grew sharp. I was raw inside from where the drugs had eaten away at me, but I was happy.

I lay on the grass with my head in your lap. You were so calm, laughing and smiling. I remember thinking we had to get out of that city as soon as possible. Maybe you could come on tour with me, or we could move somewhere else and come back for the album. You asked me what I was thinking about. I said nothing. Now I wish I'd told you exactly what was on my mind.

You stroked my hair and talked to Rapley about graffiti. Yours was another world. One with a tradition of revenge and thieves' honour. You kept trying to engage Nicholas but he showed no interest.

"I just like doing art," he'd say every so often, adjusting his straw hat.

* * *

When it grew dark, Sam and Rapley built a fire on the sand and Nicholas cooked us pasta. We ate around the flames. Again I thought of living somewhere like this, slowing everything down to a crawl.

Sam came down the beach, dragging a log behind her.

"Look what I found!" she yelled.

"Don't put that on the fire," warned Jess. Ignoring her, she hurled the log onto the flames. With a hiss, the fire went out.

"Rapley, your fire-building skills are sub-par," she said.

* * *

The next day it rained. We pulled the couches onto the deck and sat out there smoking weed. I watched the water slide off the leaves of the plants surrounding the house. The air was humid, reminding me a bit of Thailand. I had travelled there with Hayley and Jess after finishing uni. We didn't realise it was monsoon season and spent the entire time trying to keep out of the rain that never stopped.

In the early afternoon, everyone went into town to get lunch except for us. You asked if I wanted to go exploring. I would have been happy to sit inside all day, writing or talking shit. But you insisted, mumbling about how we never did anything adventurous together. You found a couple of old raincoats by the door. Yours was yellow, mine bright orange. We ventured outside, laughing at each other.

"I want to climb that hill," you said, pointing to the steep slope left of the driveway. We had to push our way through the trees and shrub to get to it. I was already sweating and out of breath by the time we got to the base of the hill.

"Maybe we should drink beer and fuck instead?" I suggested. You laughed and kissed me, then began to climb, moving easily up the hill. I followed after you, slipping on the muddy slope. I grabbed onto small trees and brushes to support myself, some of which came away in my hands, sending me sliding back down the steep bank. "This isn't dignified," I shouted after you.

When we finally got to the top, I was covered in mud and exhausted. I lay on the ground panting as the rainwater flicked my face.

"Look at that," you said. I sat up, resting on my elbows. Below us the hill led down to the ocean. The white sand was covered in driftwood. A single white row boat lay upside-down on the far end of the beach. Above it was a cliff covered in skinny, bald trees. The air smelt of earth. We sat and held hands. You were in one of your silent moods and I was still high from all the weed we smoked earlier. We watched the waves while the rain fell around us.

After fifteen minutes, we began to walk back down. Around halfway I slipped and started to run, trying to regain my balance. I crashed through bushes, picking up speed, and then fell sliding all the way to the bottom. I lay there wondering if I was hurt. I heard you walking over, laughing.

"Are you all right?" you asked between laughs.

"I think so." You reached out and helped me to my feet. Taking my hand, you led me down to the beach.

The water was still that day. You started to take off your clothes.

"I don't want to go in," I said, letting you undress me. When we were both naked you ran and threw yourself into the water.

"Come on, it's warm once you get in."

I shook my head and stood there on the shore, the rain cutting lines through the mud covering my body. You came out of the water and took my hand again.

"Come on, it's fine. Look how calm it is," you said, gently pulling me towards the sea. My stomach was tight and I realised I was holding my breath. We waded into the water. I hadn't been in the ocean since I was a teenager.

"It's okay. Relax." You were smiling, your hair pushed back off your face, you were so handsome. We walked out deeper until the water was at our chests. I hugged you as the rain fell.

"You good?" you asked. I nodded and kissed you. We were in over our heads now. Treading water.

"I've found them!" someone yelled from the shore. I turned and saw Sam. "They're fucking in the ocean!"

29 HAMISH

"YOU FUCKED JESS?"

Me and Rapley are up in the studio drinking coffee.

"Yeah, a couple of times."

"How didn't anyone notice?"

"We went down the beach."

"So no more Kate?"

"I don't know ..."

The sun's out but it's cold and the studio's empty for once. We're listening to *Blood on the Tracks*, dividing up some morphine pills we scored off Mark.

Someone's coming up the steps. I throw my jacket over the drugs.

"Hello, gentlemen." Glen walks in, looking round the place. "Looks like you've been busy."

Glen's in his early 50s but looks at least ten years younger. I don't know exactly what he does, he always seems to have half a dozen projects in the air. He's a fan of Rapley's art — always buys at least one painting every exhibition he has.

"So, how've you been?" he asks.

"Good, man," Rapley says. "Just got back from the Coromandel."

"I love that place. So this is the art for the show?"

"Yeah, most of it," I say. "Still a couple more pieces to finish up."

"Who's the girl?" Glen gestures to my work.

"Zlata. Meeting her at the café, if you wanna come have a beer?"

"You going to come too, big boy?" Glen asks Rapley.

"Yeah, why not."

* * *

Zlata's late as usual. Glen buys a bottle of wine. I tilt my glass back and forth, watching the red liquid streak down the sides.

"Sorry!" she calls from the other end of the café. "Bus didn't come."

She falls into the chair next to me, throwing her bag on the table and knocking over Rapley's glass.

"Shit." She starts wiping it up with a newspaper that was on the table.

"Don't worry 'bout it," Rapley says with a grin.

"Zlata, this is Glen."

"Hello, I'm not normally this useless. I hate walking up fucking Queen Street."

"You want a glass of wine?"

"Yes please." She hangs her jacket on the back of her chair. Her work shirt isn't ironed and there's stains on the front of it. For some reason this makes me love her more.

"Glen was telling us about his trip to Cambodia."

"Really? I went there once."

"It was a bit hairy, to be honest." Glen talks fast, waving his hands round the whole time.

"I heard it's dodgy," I say.

"I got in a fight when I was there. With a group of children."

"Children?" Zlata says.

"Yeah I had a meeting at this restaurant, and I went outside to have a smoke and this gang of kids approached me."

"How old are we talking?" she asked.

"Nine to twelve." Glen looks annoyed that his story's been interrupted.

"They were grabbing at me and asking for my money. I pushed one away and he comes back at me with a Muay Thai kick. And I thought to myself, this is a fight I can win." He finishes his glass of wine and refills it.

"So I smack one of them in the face and knee another one. I can feel his bones breaking on my knee."

"Fuck, man," Rapley says, screwing up his face.

"Afterwards there was this pile of kids. I got back up to the restaurant with blood all over me and the crazy thing was, no one seemed to care."

Zlata's staring at Glen with her mouth open.

"More wine?" he asks, holding up the bottle.

* * *

Bella and Jean are cooking us dinner. Bella's frying veggies. Jean's supposed to be making the salad. Instead, she's talking 'bout their adventures in Oz, waving her knife round. Zlata's laughing, making Jean act even more crazy. Bella tosses the vegetables, they fly up in the air and hit the pan with a hiss.

"And there was a lake filled with platypuses and ..."

"Stop lying," Bella says. Jean laughs and puts the knife down.

"Okay, there weren't platypuses, but still."

"So it was just a lake?" I ask.

"No. But there was a swimming pool," Bella giggles.

"With a dead bird in it," adds Jean.

"God, don't tell them that — it makes us sound like we got no class."

"At least I look good," Jean says, adjusting her green track suit.

"You always look good, babe."

* * *

The dinner reinforces how much me and Zlata suck at cooking.

"This is great," I say, my mouth full of food.

Bella's showing us photos of their holiday on her laptop.

"This is us in Bat Park," says Jean.

"It wasn't called that," Bella says.

"Well, it was full of bats."

"Here we are in Queensland." Bella points to a photo of her and Jean on the beach. Bella's wearing shorts and a T-shirt; Jean's dressed in a bright-green bikini, giving the thumbs up.

"Fuck, I'm hot," Jean says.

"I'm going to go out and do some painting tonight," I say to Zlata.

"Okay." I can tell she's not excited about the idea. "I won't be ages."

"It's fine," she smiles weakly.

I like the weight of the cans in my backpack.

I see Nicholas at the top of my road, pacing beneath the street lights.

"What up!" I yell, making him jump.

"Jesus," he says.

He's wearing a waistcoat over a white dress shirt. His pants are so tight it makes my balls hurt just looking at them.

We're hitting up a wall in Kingsland we've been eyeing for a couple of weeks. Nicholas keeps sighing loudly and looking around.

"What's up with you?"

"Too much coffee," he says. "Way too much."

"I thought you'd be used to it."

"Same. I got over-confident."

We walk over Bond Street Bridge. Below us a single car heads west. I stop and watch until its tail lights disappear down the motorway.

"What is it? Cops?" Nicholas asks.

"Nah, bro."

We walk the rest of the way in silence, apart from Nicholas's sighs. The image of that car stays in my head.

* * *

The wall's at the bottom of this residential street. It's in the shadows but still pretty risky. I start outlining while Nicholas walks back and forth nervously. By the time he begins, I'm halfway through my fill-in. A car drives slowly up the street and we both walk away.

"Is it gone?" he asks. I look up and down the road. Empty. We get back to work. The sickly sweet smell of spray paint fills the air. When I'm done, I step back. My piece looks good. I feel hyped till I look at what Nicholas has done. In half the time, he's made something twice as good. I throw the cans back in my backpack.

"Why've you got to be so talented?" I laugh, giving him a shove.

"Whatever, yours looks great."

We head back towards Grey Lynn.

"You excited 'bout the show?" he asks.

"I don't know, I guess."

"What I've seen looks really good."

"Hmmm."

"At least it's something to do," he says, sighing again.

28 ZLATA

THE EXORCISM BEGAN sometime in the '90s.
Most of the dead went quietly, because despite our
bravado we knew we were losers.

Why else did we live in houses filled with mouse shit
and regret, huddled in cold rooms that stank of stale time
and cigarettes?

Why else did we get high on prescription medicine and
drink ourselves into transient oblivion?

Why else did we keep having breakdowns and children,
neither of which we could afford.

Why else did we live off carcinogenic food, idolising
drunks and criminals?

Why else did we work the jobs no one else wanted, for
subsistence wages?

Why else were we responsible for all the most vile
crimes: the baby killings, the rapes and senseless beatings?

We would tell you they were symptoms of a greater
sickness. We'd quote Marx and talk revolution and social

change with surprising eloquence. But we didn't believe a word of it. Some stayed, chained to iridescent memories of home. We knew nothing else. These streets and houses were as much a part of our identity as the foreign subcultures we aligned ourselves with.

We were ready to quit a hundred dead-end jobs with obnoxious grace, write the soundtracks to this city and paint beautiful pictures on its ruins, defraud the government, sell drugs and shoplift, ready to be reduced to what we were told we always were, just to remain within its borders.

* * *

For weeks I wrestled with the idea of signing to the label. You told me I should go it alone, but a cursory glance at the people in our circles made it blindingly obvious that you had to make concessions. Otherwise you'd never get anywhere, a raw talent being worn away to nothing in some dead-end job.

In the end, it was Alice who convinced me to sign. We were drinking wine late one night, waiting for Hayley to get off work. I told her of my predicament.

"Oh, but you have to do it," she said, leaning towards me, her round face flushed from the liquor.

"It's a step forward. Maybe not as big a step as you'd wanted, but it's progress."

"But what if they make a mess of it?"

"Then you come round here and have a cry and a drink and you make another album with someone else."

"Yeah, I guess you're right."

"You'll have to start paying me by the hour for advice like this when you're a success." One of the babies started crying and she went inside.

I sat drinking, gazing out at the city. I thought of how nothing ever feels the way you think it will: love, success, travel. The nuances are always more sharp and complex than you expected. But even with this knowledge, looking back after all this time, I see none of the clutter. It's so smooth and simple. As though all I had to do was wait and everything would fall into place.

* * *

Of course I couldn't afford a lawyer. One of Jess's friends who was studying law looked over the contract.

"This isn't really my field," she said, before starting to hack at the pages with a red pen. She told me to ask for ten changes. In the end I got seven.

* * *

There was a signing party at the office. The flies were dead now, lying on their backs along the window sills. A few boxes of lukewarm beer sat on the table that had previously held the cakes. I invited you, Hayley and Fuck Yous, but of course half of Auckland showed up and things quickly descended into a shambles. Sam arrived drunk with some guy no one had met before. After telling the head of the label the beer was shit, she went and had loud sex in the toilets.

You arrived with Jamil and Skam.

"Sorry," you said when you saw me. "I couldn't lose them."

Louisa brought Nicholas. Luke and his mates appeared without explanation. Hayley came late and spent the whole time asking where the champagne was. The rep was red in the face; I thought he was going to have a heart attack.

Someone stole the fat woman's phone; Jamil threatened the rep after he asked him who he knew there. Louisa told the head of the label, a nervous, white-haired, middle-aged man, that he was a capitalist pig exploiting the creativity of the working class. It could have been worse.

27 HAMISH

THE RAIN'S SO heavy I can barely hear the stereo. Me and Rapley are sitting in his cousin's car smoking a joint. I turn the music up, can just make out Danny Brown's high-pitched ranting. Rapley takes a long drag, lowers the window and flicks the joint out into the storm.

"Should we do it?"

I throw my door open and run for the café. It's only a few metres but I'm drenched when I get inside.

"Fuck," says Rapley, shaking the rain off his jacket. A tall guy with a messy beard waves at us from one of the tables.

"Hey guys, I'm Lynton." We shake hands and sit down. "Can I get you anything?"

"Beers," I say. Rapley gives me a shove. "A couple of beers would be cool."

"Sure thing." The guy walks over to the counter. Rapley scowls at me.

"Try and hold it together a little bit."

"Sorry, that weed's real strong."

Lynton returns with some fancy beer. He pulls this stupid-looking mic from his bag and places it on the table facing us. Everyone in the café is staring. I suddenly feel self-conscious.

"If you're ready, we'll get started …"

"Sweet as."

"Okay, so the show's called *Love or Money* — can you tell me about the title?"

Rapley looks at me. I shake my head.

"It's about compromise. Compromise between your passions and getting paid. So we're doing work that reflects that." The interviewer looks at me.

"And, like, his shit's about money and mine's about love."

Rapley shakes his head.

"Why you got to go and fuck up my answer?"

I drink some beer and stare out the window at the rain. Through the glass it looks like the street is melting, running into the gutter.

"Is making money a motivation for you?"

"Well, doing a show like this it is. But you know, we'd do this shit regardless."

"I haven't made any money yet."

"What about them legal walls?" Rapley says.

"Yeah, apart from them."

"What is some of the inspiration for the show?"

"He's just painting his girlfriend over and over," Rapley laughs.

"Really?" the interviewer asks.

"Yeah," I say, still looking out the window.

"My stuff is all about how money's a bit shit."

"Can I get some more beer?" I ask.

*   *   *

The rain's stopped and a shitty-looking rainbow hangs behind the clouds. We drive along the greasy streets towards the TV3 studios. I take out one of the morphine pills and wash it down with flat Coke.

"You want one of these?" I ask, holding out the bottle.

"Aren't you wasted enough? We're going on live television, bro."

I shrug, putting the bottle back in my pocket.

"What show is it?" I ask.

"Some kinda art show, I guess."

"At 3.30 on a weekday?"

"I don't know, the publicist from the gallery hooked it up."

Rapley pulls into the parking lot. Heading into reception, my shoulder hits the door frame and I stumble, almost losing my balance. Rapley looks at me and shakes his head.

"Hey, we're here for the interview," he says to the girl behind the desk. She looks so bored she might burst into tears. She has the biggest forehead.

"Take a seat. Someone will come get you soon."

Rapley sits down. I can't stop staring at her skull.

"*Sole,*" he hisses. I turn around and he gestures to the couch. We wait in silence for ten minutes before a short woman with a headset comes out.

"Hey there, do you guys want to come through? We'll get some make-up on you."

"Make-up?" we both say at the same time.

"Yeah, just so you don't look too shiny on the TV."

"I don't wanna wear any fucking make-up," I hiss at Rapley.

"You think I do?"

We're taken into a small room with two chairs in front of a large mirror.

"Okay, if you guys can take a seat and the girls will come sort you out soon."

"What the fuck …" I say, sitting down. Rapley shrugs.

* * *

I'm too high. We're on this long couch with no back. I have to keep resting on my hands to stay upright. The make-up is making my face itchy. I feel like a dick. On my left's a skinny blonde girl who can't be much over 18. Next to Rapley's a slightly older, clean-cut, Christian-looking asshole.

"Are you all right?" the girl asks me.

"Yeah, sweet as."

"You look sick."

"It's just the make-up."

The woman with the headset comes in.

"Okay we're on in 30."

The two hosts shift in their seats.

"And 10, 9 , 8…"

I turn to Rapley.

"I think I'm going to vomit," I mutter.

"3, 2 …" The woman points at us and the hosts spring into life.

"Okay we're back and we've got some guests," the guy says, putting his arm around Rapley. Rapley shoots him a look and he pulls his arm away quickly.

"Do you want to introduce yourselves?" the girl says in a voice that borders on manic.

"Hey, I'm Rapley," he says, giving an awkward little wave. I start laughing.

"Sorry, I'm Jamil," I say. Rapley glares at me.

"So, you guys are graffiti artists?" the guy asks.

"Yeah, we mainly work with spray paint, but we use other materials too."

"So you guys do graffiti around the city?" the girl asks, smiling like a maniac.

"Yeah, sometimes. At the moment we're working towards our art show," Rapley says, trying to steer the conversation back to the exhibition.

"Do you have tags?" the guy asks.

I can tell Rapley's getting angry now. I start laughing again.

"I don't really want to talk about that."

"What advice would you give to the viewers who might be doing illegal graffiti?" the girl asks, turning to me.

"Don't be a fucking toy," I say, laughing.

"Fuck, bro," says Rapley, slapping me in the chest. I lose my balance and topple backwards off the couch, screaming with laughter.

26 ZLATA

THE EXHIBITION WAS starting to gain momentum. Posters began appearing all over town, there were articles in the paper and online and, of course, your performance on TV. You acted like you didn't care but I knew you were embarrassed. People thought of you as some kind of madman. But in truth, when sober, you were reserved, more likely to fade into the background than do something outlandish. You began leaving for the studio at seven in the morning, I suspect so you didn't have to bump into anyone that was going to hassle you. But your friends were only too happy to seek you out.

Sam was the most vocal, turning up at the studio, drinking beers and berating you.

"Made quite the spectacle of yourself, didn't you? You'd think at your age you could handle your piss."

You would silently continue painting.

* * *

Around the same time, my album began to take shape. By the week of the exhibition I had ten solid songs and another two on the way. The month was filled with excitement. I floated through the city on those rusty autumn afternoons. Even work couldn't bring me down. I just smiled and ignored everyone while I uploaded pictures of geriatric women on Hayley's page. When the days became lazy and began to move slowly, I would think of the album and you and this new life that had grown up out of the wreckage of the old.

The label wanted a radio song, of course. While most of the tracks were catchy enough, I still didn't have one that screamed 'single'. It was hard to write honestly about your life and squeeze it into the confines of a three-minute pop structure. I was sitting in our bedroom when it came to me. It might have been late night or early morning; either way it was dark. At first I just had the phrase, 'Everything happens for a stupid reason' — it was something Luke came up with. Me and him were out on Louisa's deck working on songs. I was playing a new riff I really liked while he talked about his and his friends' adventures.

"And then the cops came and we were hiding in this bush and fucking Freckles' phone goes off." We laughed while I kept playing. "We got away, though. Everything happens for a stupid reason."

And so I sat in my room playing that riff over and over. The only light was from my lamp and in the dark I hit the wrong chord. It jarred against the melodic progression of the riff. I held the chord for a while and then went back into the riff. The juxtaposition made the progression even catchier. Then I started rambling some ideas over the chord and made it the verse. I talked about me and you, the label, work, our friends; all the ridiculous things that had happened over those six months that had made life a little more interesting. I sang 'Everything happens for a stupid reason' over the main riff. It sounded good, but if you'd told me what was going to happen I'd never have believed you.

25 HAMISH

THE VIDEO GOT 20,000 hits on YouTube. Every time I go outside some dickhead yells, "Don't be a fucking toy." I'm going to punch someone soon. Rapley can't decide if this is good or bad publicity.

"The gallery aren't impressed, but I reckon people gonna come."

"It's doing my head in."

I'm working on the last couple of paintings. Rapley's already finished all his pieces.

"It's your own fault, brother," he says, rolling a joint.

Looking at his paintings, I am filled with doubt. His lines are so clean; his ideas clever. It seems with each painting my work keeps getting stranger. It's been fun though, stepping away from the stress of dealing, waking up every morning knowing all I got to do is head to the studio and paint. Someone from the gallery's coming by this afternoon to look at the works and talk about hanging them. My stomach hurts.

"Hey there." The woman's dressed like she's going to a funeral. Rich people are so weird.

"Hey, Linda," Rapley hugs her. "This is Hamish."

"Do you know someone's written 'I'm going to kill you' on the door downstairs?"

"Maybe that's what we should've called the show," Rapley laughs.

"That's funny," Linda says, without smiling.

Rapley leads her to his corner of the studio and starts showing her his pieces.

"These are great; they have a lot of impact. Have you thought about pricing?"

"Yeah, I was thinking two grand for the big ones, five hundred for the smaller ones."

"I'd ask for a bit more, but we can talk about that later." She turns and heads over to me. My hands are shaking. I put down my brush and lean on the table. She looks the paintings up and down without saying anything for ages.

"This is great work," she says finally. "I mean, the progression from realism to abstraction is really clever. It's a very interesting take on the flux of emotions within relationships. Where did you study?" she says, turning to face me. I look at Rapley; he's grinning like an idiot.

"I went to Springs."

"No, after high school."

"Nowhere."

She turns and looks at the work again. "Well, I think we've got ourselves a really strong show."

* * *

"And then she was like, 'Where did you study?', like I went to uni or some shit." We're crowded round the kitchen table at home, drinking beers.

"Baby, you see? I told you your art's amazing."

"Excuse me, I was the one that convinced him to pick up a paint brush," says Rapley.

"Oh, we're competing for him are we?" Zlata jumps up, holding out an empty bottle. Rapley throws up his hands.

"You can have him."

She sits down and opens another beer.

"To the show." She holds her drink up.

"To a couple of losers doing good." We clink bottles.

"So only two more days," says Bella. "It's all go at the moment."

"Are you hanging it tomorrow?" Zlata asks.

"Yeah, in the afternoon. Got to head out south and try to convince the family to come in." Rapley says.

"Why wouldn't they?"

"They just don't come to shit like this usually." Rapley turns to me. "You still coming out? Auntie was asking about you."

* * *

"Where the fuck is it …" We're at the bus stop on Symonds Street. It's starting to rain.

"It says eight minutes on the GPS thing," I say, pointing at the sign.

"Yeah, it said six minutes just before. Is it fucking driving backwards?"

We've been at this bus stop for over half an hour.

"Twelve minutes? What the fuck."

I offer him one of the morphine pills.

"Nah man, that stuff will make you constipated."

I swallow one and lean back on the glass shelter.

"Look, now it says delayed." Rapley kicks the side of the bus stop.

* * *

Onehunga shopping centre looks like Grey Lynn did back in the day. A random bunch of shops along the main street, butchers next to bookstores next to two-dollar shops. The street's real busy despite the weather. I thought about moving here, but it's too far from everyone and everything. We walk up the street past a group of young dickheads outside the WINZ. They all start whispering as we go past.

"Here it comes," I say.

"Don't be a fucking toy!" one of them yells after us. They burst out laughing. I stop and turn around.

"What?" the biggest dude yells. They all take a couple of steps forward.

"Come on, they're just kids" says Rapley, pulling me away by my arm.

"Yeah, you better run, faggot."

"You're a real celebrity," Rapley laughs.

* * *

Auntie's smiling frame fills the doorway. Two small boys peek around her thick legs.

"Hello," she says, giving Rapley a strong hug. "And Hamish." She squeezes the air out of me.

"Look how skinny you are," she pokes at my stomach.

We walk into the living room. Rapley's cousin Peter and his three sons are watching TV.

"Hey, bro," Peter says, getting up and slapping our hands. He's a kickboxer, just turned pro. His first professional fight lasted 30 seconds — all it took for him to beat his opponent to a pulp. His arms are the size of my calves. Rapley picks up all three of his nephews at the same time.

"How are yous?"

They struggle, laughing and kicking their feet. He puts them down and we join Auntie in the kitchen.

"Are you on the dole again?" she says to me. "Is that why you're wasting away?"

"No, Auntie," I say, laughing.

"His girlfriend is a vegetarian," Rapley says. Auntie breathes out through her teeth.

"That's why." She goes to fridge. "I'll cook you some real food."

She gets out a packet of bacon and some eggs.

"So, did you get the invite to the art show I'm doing?"

"Yes, it's on the fridge," she says, pointing.

"So, are you going to come?"

"I don't know. It's hard getting to town."

"I'll get Denny to come pick you up."

"I don't know."

Rapley goes into the lounge.

"Peter, come in here." The kitchen's suddenly very crowded.

"I was saying to Auntie that I want yous to come to the show."

"What about the boys?" Peter says.

"They can come too; there'll be heaps of kids."

Peter shakes his head, "I don't know, I got training."

Rapley sighs.

"Is your family coming, Hamish?" Auntie asks me.

"I don't think so."

"See," she says.

"Yeah, but his family is crazy, no offence."

"It's okay."

The smell of frying bacon fills the kitchen.

"Food's ready," says Auntie.

24 ZLATA

THE DAY OF the art show opening, I called in sick to work. I was going to do a short set along with Luke's rap group. Me and Jean sat on the front steps of the house and ate breakfast. We watched the traffic and talked while the anaemic sun did its best to warm us. Jean told me she'd won some competition recently. She was so casual about everything it could have been the Olympics or a running race with Bella at the park.

Of course I talked about the single. The demo sat on my laptop, and every hour or so I played it again to make sure it was still breathing. Watching the street flow past, framed in the gold of autumn leaves, my stomach burning with excitement, I thought how that city was like a dead love. One day you wake up next to a stranger that slightly repels you and realise the person you fell in love with has died. Over time you work up the courage to pack your things, bury them and go stay with your mother. Then they turn around and kiss you like they did when they were alive.

And you think, 'Am I crazy'? How could I leave this? So you stay for another day, week, month, year. That autumn I fell back in love with Grey Lynn, and had things not gone the way they did that night, maybe I'd still be there now.

* * *

I caught a taxi to the gallery with my gear. The pot holes in the road were so bad I thought the suspension would snap any minute. I unloaded my stuff and waded ankle-deep through rubbish to the entrance. It was empty, apart from the pictures hanging on the sparse white walls. Rapley's work was cartoon-influenced, his art depicting scenes of excess and greed. Half-human creatures rolled around in pools of money and shit. Everything was busy and screaming. The images seemed to follow me.

Your work was much gentler. What a strange sensation, looking at 12 portraits of myself, each less refined than the last. When you reached the end it was a mess of colours around a silhouette of me.

"You're the girl from the painting," someone said. I turned and saw a tall, androgynous woman with a clipboard standing very close.

"Yeah, Hamish is my boyfriend."

"Okay. Well, what do you think?" Both her words and face were expressionless; my own words began to dissolve on my tongue.

"Umm … yeah, it's cool …" She smiled ever so slightly then walked over to Rapley's work and put a red sticker next to one of the paintings.

"Someone's already bought this one."

"Wow." I looked at my pile of battered gear. "I'm supposed to be playing here later. Where do you want me to set up?" The woman tilted her head and looked at me as if I had asked a question of the utmost importance.

"Wherever you want," she said eventually, and walked away.

I started fiddling with the drum machine. It kept turning itself off for no apparent reason. You and Rapley came in carrying boxes of beer.

"Hey, beautiful," you said, setting the alcohol down and kissing me.

"Are you worried about the weather?" I asked.

You looked outside.

"No, why?"

Suddenly the drum machine came on with a loud pop. "Bingo!" I said, clapping my hands.

* * *

Outside the gallery, the weather soured. We had dinner at some Indian restaurant down the road. The storm was making me anxious and I struggled to eat. It didn't faze you; nothing really did. I watched you wash down your curry with beer, laughing at Rapley's stories.

When we left the restaurant the street was desolate. I picked at a hole in the sleeve of my hoodie as I stood outside among the dancing rubbish. I could feel something brewing, a sense of anticipation. Things had been building so long there had to be a release. You and Rapley were laughing, pushing into the wind as I trailed behind. The power lines sparked above us. In the distance was a light filled with people shouting and drinking.

"Wow, look at that," you said, quickening your pace as we crossed the street. When we reached the gallery we were enveloped. It was overwhelming. It seemed like everyone

I'd ever met was there, all reaching out and grabbing at us, making small talk into my face. I pushed my way inside and checked on my gear. You came up to me.

"I've sold six paintings!" you said. I hugged you. Over your shoulder, a hundred faces leered at us and I clutched you tight.

I was standing with Sam and Hayley when Luke's rap group started playing.

"This is for everyone who didn't finish school," Luke yelled.

"Ahh, fuck this," Sam said, walking outside.

The beat dropped and Luke and his mates started chanting, 'I'm a fucking genius', while stumbling around, tripping over the mic leads.

"These are your friends?" Hayley asked, raising her eyebrows. I gave her playful push.

"I can't believe how many people are here," she said in my ear. "I guess going on TV wasted wasn't the worst idea after all." I looked over at you, standing by your paintings with a huge smile while people vied for your attention. That guy Glen was there, pointing to a painting he wanted to buy.

I hugged Hayley.

"Let's go get a drink," I said, pulling her towards the back of the gallery.

"You two will be a real power couple if this keeps up."

I let out an empty laugh. I was distracted by the storm. Rain beat against the windows, wind howled over the top of the music. Alice came over with the older of her two children.

"How exciting is this?" she said, picking up a glass of wine. "So many people and the art is amazing."

"I was just saying Hamish and Zlata will be a celebrity couple soon."

"Is there anything more depressing than a New Zealand celebrity?"

"Take my photo with Z!" Jean said, throwing her long muscular arms around me.

"I'm supposed to be taking photos for the magazine," Bella said.

"They will love photos of me."

Bella sighed and snapped a couple of shots.

"Look, there's the star of the show," Jean exclaimed, pushing her way through the crowd to where you were standing, a beer in each hand. Bella rolled her eyes and followed after her.

"When are you playing?" someone said behind me. I turned and saw Nicholas. He was wearing a silver suit, his hair slicked back.

"Hey, you. Soon, I think."

"Exciting." He ran his fingers through his hair. "You've been so positive for Hamish," he said, looking me in the eye.

"I don't know about that," I said, turning away, embarrassed by the sincerity in his voice.

"I'm serious. A year ago I could have never have imagined him doing something like this."

"Thanks." I sipped my wine.

"Well, anyway, it's great. I'm so proud."

Behind him, faces pressed up to the glass.

* * *

It happened while I was playing. I was halfway through my second or third song when the crowd started turning and staring outside. I kept playing until people began screaming.

I dropped my guitar and pushed my way through the crowd, so heavy I could barely lift my feet.

Outside, you, Rapley and half a dozen other people stood in a circle looking at something on the footpath. When I reached you, I saw a guy lying in a pool of blood, Luke's hunting knife next to him. Nobody was doing anything; they all just stood there in the wind, their faces pale and expressionless. I knelt down next to the guy and felt his pulse — it was still. I heard sirens and the circle dissipated. Someone grabbed my arm and the next thing we were running.

23 HAMISH

"WHERE'S LUKE?" Rapley keeps saying.

We're back at his house. People are turning up, shocked and out of breath. Everyone crowds into the living room. No one's seen Luke; he's not answering his phone.

"We should go look for him," Zlata says. She has blood on her jeans and arms.

"Nah, we should wait," Rapley snaps.

"The cops are going to come here sooner or later; they know it was your show."

"Maybe the cops already got him," says Nicholas.

"Fuck. I told him to get rid of that fucking knife how many times?"

"We should go look for him," Zlata says again.

"You fucking go if you want," Rapley says.

"Don't talk to her like that," I say, shoving him.

The door slowly opens. Everyone turns. Luke is standing in the doorway, covered in blood.

"I'm sorry," he keeps saying.

Rapley gives him a mug of whisky.

"It's okay," he says, even though it's obviously not.

Zlata is next to Luke on the couch. She puts her arm around him and he starts crying. I should sit with him but I can't. I feel like I'm going to be sick.

"Shhhh," she says, stroking his head. Rapley grabs me by the arm and pulls me into the hallway. He looks like he's in pain, his eyes wide.

"What should we do?" he asks. "The cops are going to know it's him, half of Auckland saw him do it."

"We should let him sleep, then take him to the cops tomorrow," I say.

Rapley starts pacing up and down the hallway.

"You think?" His voice breaks a little. "Fuck!" He slams his fist against the wall.

* * *

Luke passes out after a couple of mugs of whisky. We leave him on the couch and gather round the kitchen table.

"What the fuck happened?" asks Zlata.

"It's this crew we had beef with," Rapley says. After what's just happened, his words sound stupid and petty.

"They tried to fight us out front," I say. "Heaps of them. They all took off after Luke stabbed their mate."

Skam, who's standing back by the sink drinking out of a bottle of vodka, laughs. Everyone glares at him.

"You know he's going to go to jail, right?" Zlata says.

"I tried to take that knife off him like ten times," I say. "None of us carry knives."

"He was just drunk, showing off," Rapley says.

"Well, I don't think that's going to help him in court."

Everyone goes quiet.

* * *

It's late. Me and Rapley are sitting on his porch smoking a joint. The others are inside watching movies.

"Poor guy," I say, passing him the weed. Rapley takes a drag and says nothing. A car drives slowly past and I watch it retreat up Dryden Street.

* * *

The next morning we head to the police station at eight. Luke doesn't say a word. We park on Hobson Street by Wah Lee's and walk down. Zlata holds his hand. Me and Rapley hang back while they approach the front desk. I know Rapley hates being here. He's always on that 'fuck cops' shit. I hate them too, but they have their job and I got mine.

"This is bullshit," I say. "We've got to find him a lawyer, can't leave him to those legal aid clowns."

"What about his folks?"

"His dad's gone and his mum's nuts."

"Fuck, okay, let's go suss that after he's booked."

Zlata and Luke walk back over with a cop following close behind.

"They're taking him in now," Zlata says.

Luke is staring at the ground. I give him a hug. He feels so small, I wish I could go in there instead of him.

"We're going to go find you a lawyer now, bro."

Luke nods, his eyes look scared.

"Don't say shit to them till we get someone," Rapley says.

They hug and then we leave.

Outside, Zlata bursts into tears. I hold her while Rapley slumps down against the wall.

22 ZLATA

THE WEEKS FOLLOWING the show were stubborn. We found a lawyer and pooled our money. Because Luke was 17, they held him in a borstal. That place was like nightmares in hospital waiting rooms. We went to see him with the lawyer, a small man with an aggressive practicality.

"Best we can hope for is manslaughter," he said on our first meeting. I asked him to dress the situation up for Luke, but when they met it was one of the first things he said. Luke looked at us as though we would contradict the lawyer. I fought the urge to look away. We brought him food and books. After the lawyer finished talking, we tried to discuss things other than the case. It was like talking about the weather in a burning house. We gave him the gifts and he pushed them back across the table.

"The others will just take them," he said. So we sat and ate cake and fruit with him until it was time to leave.

During this period you barely talked. We were both broke: I was waiting for the advance from the record company and you still hadn't been paid from the exhibition. In the meantime, we lived off my wages and what you shoplifted. I tried to talk about what had happened but you just drank and swallowed pills, staring at something I couldn't see. People blamed you for what happened. That city was like that: there always had to be a scapegoat.

"You didn't do anything wrong," I told you. "You tried to help him so many times."

"Yeah," you'd say, staring at whatever was haunting you.

* * *

After a week, with things showing no sign of improving. I went to see Louisa. We had a picnic out the back of her house with Sam and the kids. The yard was overgrown, trees wrapped themselves around the house and the fence. We ate in the shade of a lemon tree. The children grabbed at the food and ran into the wilderness.

"How's Hamish?" Louisa asked.

I shrugged.

"Not good. He feels really guilty."

"Yeah, some people were talking shit when I was out last night," Sam said.

"That's just this place though," said Lou. "He knows that."

"It's Luke I'm really worried about," I said.

"Yeah. Prison isn't going to be kind to him." Sam said, throwing the crust from her sandwich into the bushes.

We sat listening to the children yelling and screaming in the distance.

* * *

The cops wanted to talk to us. You avoided them for as long as possible, but eventually I made you come to the station with me.

"This is just a stupid fucking game they play," you said as we walked over Hopetoun Bridge.

The sergeant in charge of the case was a fast-talking half-wit. I was surprised how rude and condescending he was, trying to trip us up with his clumsy questioning. You said nothing other than yes or no the entire interview, refusing to make eye contact.

"Are we suspects?" I asked at one point.

"No, why should you be?"

You were visibly shaken after the interview. As soon as we got home you climbed into bed and refused to talk.

* * *

We had an appointment to visit Luke but you disappeared, leaving your phone behind. I caught the bus out alone. It was empty, apart from a scruffy child who kept looking at me, his head snapping back around whenever our eyes met. I watched the suburbs change as we headed south: the houses less uniform, the strips of shops more chaotic. I got off at the wrong stop and had to walk for 20 minutes to reach the large grey building.

After checking in, I waited on a hard plastic chair. Every part of me was screaming 'get out', but I thought of Luke. He would be in places worse than this until he was my age. The least I could do was distract him for half an hour. He was led out and sat opposite me, wearing a black eye.

"Hey." He looked at me with his head still facing the

table. It reminded me of you. We talked about the case for a little bit, then I told him how I was going to record the album soon.

"I really don't want to be here," he said, cutting me off. I got up and hugged him. I wanted to say something reassuring but what was there to say?

* * *

You came home late, drunk, covered in dirt and paint.

"Sorry," you slurred. You started to pull off your clothes. "Sorry," you said again.

"You have to go see him; he isn't good."

"Sorry."

You climbed into bed. Your hands burnt when you touched me and I pushed them away.

"I'm worried about him."

"Don't."

"How can you talk like that?"

"Sorry."

"Stop fucking saying that."

"He killed someone. I can't do anything!" you yelled.

I lay among the silence, feeling seasick.

21 HAMISH

"BUT I DON'T have $400."

"You have a credit card."

Priscilla's washing lettuce in the sink. She stops, stares at me with tired brown eyes. "You think I'm going to get myself further into debt so you can get high?"

"It's not for drugs. I just need some cash for food."

Priscilla goes back to washing the lettuce. I take a sip of my beer. It's warm and makes me feel sick. "I can pay you back when I get paid from the show."

"Why don't you ask your dad?" she says, not turning from the sink. This isn't a question – just a polite way of telling me to fuck off. I finish the beer and get up from the table.

"Okay, well, thanks anyway, Mum." I toss the bottle into the rubbish.

"Don't call me that, and put the bottle in the bloody recycling!" she yells after me.

I never talk about my dad much. He wasn't really there

even before he left. Always drunk or at work on the docks, always angry about some bullshit, always yelling and then … gone. And Mum wasn't the most loving person either. I don't think she'd ever wanted a kid. She'd have preferred to keep the party going rather than worry about nappies and shopping for food.

After he left, shit got worse. She hit the bottle for real. I started living at Rapley's. Anyway …

* * *

Rapley's cousin Denny is playing some first-person shooter. Everything's exploding and dying. I'm waiting for Rapley. He texted, said to be at his at 3 p.m., that he had some news. It was 3.30 p.m. and he still wasn't here. I pop another morphine pill and watch the ultra-violence on the screen in a warm daze till Rapley finally turns up.

"What up," he says, slapping my hand. "Come in my room."

I lie on his bed and stare at the art on the walls.

"Don't put your shoes on the blanket," he says, sitting down at his desk. "How you been?"

"I don't know. Feel like I'm going crazy."

"It's fucked up," he starts rolling a joint. "Out of all the boys, Luke was the last one I thought would do something like that."

"Have you been to see him?" I ask.

"Not this week. Me and Denny are heading out tomorrow. Wanna come?"

"Nah, I got shit on." Rapley gives me a look and then sparks the joint.

"So I saw Linda and she's going to deposit that money next week."

"Thank fuck."

"And she said we got asked to be part of a group show in Tokyo."

I sit up.

"You serious?"

"Yeah, in a couple of weeks. We have to pay for the flights, but everything else is taken care of."

I lie down again.

"That's crazy."

"We need to let her know by tomorrow." He passes me the joint. I take a hit and think about Luke. I've been in places like that before. Only for a couple of months at a time, but it was bad enough.

You have to grow up real fast once you're in the system. Me and Rapley went in together. We never really talk about what happened in there, but I know it's on his mind.

"I'm down," I say.

"You don't need to talk to Zlata?"

"I will when I get home."

* * *

I meant to go home after Rapley's – I really did. Instead, I ended up wandering in a drug haze through the park. Thinking about the same shit. Flashbacks of ten years ago. I've never been as scared as that first day, walking out into the yard, and I've been taking and giving beatings since I could walk.

"Yo yo," someone calls from the shadows.

I turn and see Jamil and Skam on their bench.

"Hey," I say, walking over.

"Heard that little pussy stabbed up one of them DMT faggots."

I say nothing and take a seat.

"Have a beer." Skam thrusts a can at me.

"You must be rich now you're a famous artist."

"Hardly."

"I heard you sold heaps."

"Yeah, haven't got any money yet but ..."

"We're flush, aren't we bro?" Jamil says to Skam.

"Rich as."

"Sold off all that shit you gave me." He opened another can. "It's a seller's market." Jamil starts laughing, spilling his beer.

"What you going to do with the money?"

"Spend it, baby."

We sit in the park drinking while Jamil goes off on one of his rants.

* * *

When I get home, Zlata's asleep. It's been like this for the last week. I almost wake her and tell her about Japan, but she's got work tomorrow. I get a beer out of the fridge and sit on the front steps, trying not to think about Luke.

20 ZLATA

WHEN THE ADVANCE came through I bought my first proper meal in two weeks. I ate alone in an empty restaurant. A transistor radio played Vietnamese pop music in a storm of static. You had told me about Japan the night before. I stood there unable to speak. When I finally did, my words came out cluttered.

"But we're broke. And Luke's trial is coming up. And I'm doing my album." You simply stared at me until I hit you as hard as I could in the face. And then you left.

The next day Sam helped me load my stuff into the recording studio. It was an old theatre filled with vintage gear and the smell of damp carpet. Sam played drums on the album. I was excited; it was the first time I'd used a live drummer. The label wanted to get the song out as soon as possible. Jason the engineer looked at my collection of half-broken equipment through his sex-offender glasses and shook his head.

"You want to record an album with this?" He gestured

at my gear with one of his chubby hands.

"I guess." He shook his head again and started pulling out mics and leads.

"What's his problem?" Sam asked, walking over.

"Nothing. Set up your drums," I said, fearing an incident. I went out to the street and tried your phone. You were leaving tomorrow. The sound of drums echoed through the building.

"Hey." I could tell by the tone in your voice that you'd been taking drugs again.

"Where are you?"

"Just out."

"I want to see you tonight before you go."

"I'll be home."

"I love you."

"Yeah, me too."

I hung up and went back down into the gloom.

* * *

We got the takes quickly. With real drums the song had a new urgency. When it came time to do my vocals I stepped eagerly to the mic. The words knew their place and I didn't need to hear the playback to know I'd nailed it. I got Sam to yell in the background of the hook. By late afternoon the song was done and Jason gave me a rough mix of the track to take home. We decided to walk back to Grey Lynn, even though it was over an hour away. We talked about Japan and the album and Luke. It was like the three things were somehow linked by more than bad timing.

"I'm going to go see him tomorrow," Sam said. "Nicholas is giving him one of his suits for the trial."

"Tell him I'll be out after recording's done."

"Sure."

We walked down Dominion Road, past the Asian restaurants and cell phone stores. Everything burned bright against the dusk. The street was busy, traffic backed up in either direction. I took Sam's hand, my guitar in the other and we headed into the winter's night.

* * *

You were waiting for me at home. You'd stolen a bottle of my favourite wine and handed it to me with a smile dripping off your face. Your right eye was nestled in a rotten bruise. We hugged and I hoped the chill that sat in my chest would melt.

"Do you want to hear the song?" I asked, as you stared at me from beneath heavy eyelids.

"Of course." You were always so gentle when you were high. We drank the wine and listened to my song on repeat.

"I'm so cold," I said, when the bottle was empty.

"Let's get into bed."

We took off our clothes and tried to fuck, but neither of us had the energy. Instead we lay there in silence. I fought the urge to talk. I didn't want your sickly apologies and excuses climbing into bed with us.

* * *

The next morning I woke up late for my studio session.

"Wake up, baby," I kept saying while I stumbled round the room trying to find my clothes. I ended up having to shake you.

"I have to go." You wiped your face and stared blankly at me.

"I'm not going to see you for a week," I said.

You pulled me back into bed and held on tight.

19 HAMISH

ZLATA'S GONE. I can kinda remember saying good-bye. I think about calling her but she'll be recording. Pushing my way through the drug mist, I climb into the shower; my thoughts slowly warm up. Rapley will be here soon and I haven't even packed. He's got the canvasses, which is the main thing. I get out and look at myself in the filthy mirror. I've lost weight. My hair is looking wild, like it always does after a few months' neglect. I eat breakfast and Luke pops into my head. It's like the look he gave me in that cell is burnt into my brain. Feeling around in my pockets, I find my last two morphine pills and swallow them both.

* * *

"What happened to your face?" I clutch my boarding pass and try and keep from nodding off.

"Zlata punched me," I say, feeling my eyes close.

Rapley shoves me.

"Wait till we get on the plane before you pass out."

I sit up.

"You think Luke will be okay?"

Rapley looks at me like I'm crazy. "No."

"Neither."

"This exhibition's a big deal."

"Yeah."

"We got to do it. You should've gone seen him before we left."

"I know."

"When we get back we'll both go visit."

I feel my eyes closing again.

"I just think, you know … him in there …" I mutter.

"Fuck, bro, I gave all my money for that lawyer and I talked to some of the boys inside. They gonna look after him, all right?" People are staring at us now.

"We are now boarding rows 18 to 35," a voice says over the speaker.

"That's us." Rapley pulls me to my feet with one hand.

* * *

At the hotel's reception a language barrier, our tattoos and me not being able to stand unassisted lead to a commotion. Eventually we're taken to our room. I fall onto my bed and drift into a coma filled with sex dreams and confusion. When I wake up, it's dark. I look out the window. Down on the street everything is burning and moving. I call Rapley.

"You're up."

"Yeah, where are you?"

"At the gallery. Get in a taxi – I'll text you the address."

My clothes stink of sweat. I pull them on and drink

water out of the tap. On the street the air's hot and thick, so different from home. People push past me. I look around for a taxi but there's none. My phone beeps: Rapley with the address. Coming down off the drugs and it's dawning on me — I'm in fucking Japan! In all my life I never thought I'd go somewhere like this. People are pushing past me on all sides. I'm scared to be sober. I'm already getting that dark, heavy feeling. I buy a couple of beers and drain them both. Eventually I'm in a green cab. I text Zlata: "In Japan, miss you."

* * *

The gallery's on the 7th floor of an office building. I don't trust the lift so I take the stairs and stumble panting into a large room filled with boxes; canvasses hang or are propped against the wall. Rapley's standing in one corner with a Japanese man in a suit and waves me over.

"This is Takumi, he's curating the show." I put my hand out, he bows, then I bow. He goes to shake my hand.

"You sleep well?" he asks, after the greeting fiasco's sorted.

"Yeah, man." I look round the gallery. Some works have already been hung. Their shit's mostly stolen off more famous artists. I feel confident 'bout the ones we brought.

"Takumi is going to show us around tonight."

"Choice." I need to keep drinking.

"I think the show will be popular," Takumi says as we walk down the street. "We have had a lot of success in the last year." He leads us down an alley and through a small door that opens out into a giant restaurant.

We order these fucking huge jugs of beer each, much to the amusement of our guide.

"You like beer?" he asks.

"Yeah, bro."

"Then you will like Tokyo."

I drink out of the jug. Rapley gives me one of his judgmental looks.

Takumi orders for us. Small plates filled with different-coloured seafood and meat are brought out. I struggle to use the chopsticks. In the end I give up and eat with my hands. Rapley acts like he's cultured and soldiers on. What a couple of hicks.

* * *

After dinner we wander the streets of Tokyo. My legs are weak from the beer and jetlag.

"How crazy is this place," I say, overwhelmed by the buildings and lights.

"I can't get over all the people," Rapley says, towering above the crowds.

"You should come here in the day," says Takumi. "Many more people."

"I think that would stress me out," I say, bumping into someone.

18 ZLATA

THE REST OF the album was harder than the single. I struggled with my vocals. Jason wanted things to be pitch-perfect and kept deleting takes without me hearing them back.

"It's part of my sound," I told him. In truth, it was hard to sing those songs with you so far away. But I was younger then, not just in years, and I let him control the sessions.

Sam had laid down her drum parts so most of the days were spent with only me and Jason in that cavernous studio. By the third day, I was dreading the next session. Now on the rare occasion I listen to those recordings I can hear it in my voice. In a sadistic way, I think it actually makes it better. There is an urgency there, I am pushing myself to get the parts done, no longer able to remove myself in any way. But at the time it sounded like me losing my mind. The single was mixed and mastered. The label weren't 100 percent about it but had nothing else. I would be making a video the day before Luke's court hearing. It was getting hard to breathe.

* * *

Me, Jess and Hayley met up for dinner after day four. My voice was cracked and my eyes burned.

"You look like absolute shit," said Hayley when I sat down with her.

"Thanks."

"No, you really do." She stroked my face, her long plastic nails scraping against my cheeks. "What have you been doing?"

"Making music."

"I thought it was supposed to be fun."

"It's fine."

Jess exploded through the door and flew over to our table. She dropped her comically large bag and fell into a seat.

"Okay, fuck this day," she said, picking up Hayley's wine and finishing it in one go. "It can suck my dick."

"What's up?" Hayley asked, filling another glass.

"So my intern can't even use Microsoft Word, one of the clients just rejected my prop that I've been working on for two weeks, and I just got a fucking parking ticket." She grabbed the bottle and took another drink.

"Try to have a little decorum," Hayley said.

"What's wrong with you?" Jess asked, turning to face me. "You look like you've been smoking crack."

"Making an album."

We sat in silence while Jess looked at the menu. I could feel Hayley watching me.

"What the fuck happened at the show?" Hayley asked,

surprising me with the concern in her voice. "I was talking to some guy and then everyone started screaming."

"I heard that friend of Hamish's killed someone," Jess said, putting down the menu.

"Let's not talk about it, please," I said, trying not to cry.

Jess and Hayley exchanged glances.

"Sorry, Zlata, but I'm going to eat something with heaps of meat in it," Jess said.

* * *

Afterwards the three of us drank on Hayley's porch. It was cold and we sat under a duvet, passing a bottle of red wine back and forth.

"Where's Alice?" I asked. I was drunk and found myself holding Jess's hand beneath the blanket.

"With the kids and their dad," Hayley said absent-mindedly. She was glued to her phone.

"It's cool they still get along."

"He's a nice guy." The screen shone a blue light onto her heavily made-up face.

"Do you ever think about having kids?" Jess asked.

"Fuck no," says Hayley, still not looking up from her phone. "I can't stand them."

"I always thought I would but now I'm not so sure," I said. "I don't know if it's fair on them."

"I want heaps," said Jess. "Just need to make lots of money first." She squeezed my hand and I leant into her soft shoulder.

"I'm making a video next week," I mumbled.

"Your life's very exciting," said Jess.

"I don't know about that. Stressful's a better word."

"That's what excitement is."

"You get so bored when nothing dramatic is happening," said Hayley, passing the bottle back to me. "You always have to have a million tiny disasters in your life."

Something moved in the tree in front of us, making me jump. A possum ran out on the end of a branch and looked at me with its glassy black eyes.

* * *

Back in the studio I struggled through the rest of the album. Jason insisted on taking a two-hour break every day at 1 p.m. Since it was too far to go home, I'd use this time to climb Mt Eden and rework lyrics. I sat under the same tree, crossing out phrases and honing my thoughts, while below me the city churned. When I returned to the studio we'd begin again. A couple of times the label rep came by. He would listen to the sessions, nodding along, out of time, with a stupid grin on his face. Then he'd say something pithy and leave. The only thing me and Jason bonded over was our dislike for him.

"That guy doesn't even like music," he said, narrowing his little rat eyes.

By week's end the album was recorded. I went home on Saturday night exhausted and filled with dread. It was going to be awful, I thought. My voice was shot and we had eaten into the promo budget. I tried to Skype you but you weren't online. I fell asleep early and woke up to a text: "Show was a failure."

"Come online."

"Can't. Lost in Tokyo," you replied.

17 HAMISH

THE HOTEL ROOM looks like we've been using it to house wild dogs. We don't want to let the cleaners in 'cos we've lost a bag of coke in here somewhere. You have to walk over dirty clothes and empty bottles to get from the beds to the bathroom. One of the Japanese women Rapley's been fucking is passed out on his bed. He's throwing things around, trying to find his phone. I'm waiting for Zlata to come online so we can Skype.

"Where the fuck is it?" he groans, kicking his suitcase. My laptop's ringing.

"Hey you." Zlata's face fills the screen. She looks tired.

"Can you see me?"

"No ... wait ... there you are." We both stare at each other, smiling.

"How was the show?"

"Sucked, didn't sell anything."

"How come?"

"I don't know, guess they weren't into my shit."

"That sucks, but you'll get other shows."

Rapley chucks the suitcase across the room. It hits the wall, making the Japanese girl sit up with a start.

"Who's that?" Zlata asks.

"Masako?"

The girl looks at me. "No, I am Tamako."

"Sorry."

She walks over and leans into the screen. "Is this your wife, the famous one?"

"Hello, I'm Zlata."

"Oh, that's a nice name. Are you in Australia?"

"We're from New Zealand," Rapley snaps. "I told you like ten times."

"It's the same."

"No, it's like saying Japan is Korea."

The girl says something in Japanese and shuffles back to Rapley's bed.

"How's the album?"

"It's okay. The single's getting lots of play on the radio, which I guess is good."

"Sweet."

We both go quiet. I can hear Jean and Bella having sex in the background. Zlata starts laughing. "I bet you miss listening to that every night." She gets up, walks off screen and returns with a piece of paper. It's a photo of one of my paintings of her, where the colours wash into one another. "I want to use this as the album cover," she says.

"Really?"

"Is that cool?"

"Of course."

"Cool. So you got lost?"

"I don't want to talk about it."

"I do," says Rapley grabbing the laptop off me. "Hey, Zlata."

"Rapley, how are you?"

"Good, good. So the other night we have the show and Hammy has too much to drink. We head out after with the curator and a couple of the artists to some bar … What was the name of that place?" he asks me. "Fuck, how would you know. We're doing shots of this spirit that has a snake in the bottle."

"A real snake?"

"Yeah."

"That's fucked."

"I know, this place is worse than the islands for vegetarians. Anyway, everyone's dancing and whatever and then there's this ruckus and Hamish is arguing with the owner of the bar. So I go over with the curator to see what's up. The owner is screaming at him in Japanese and Hamish just keeps yelling *arigato* over and over. Turns out he's tagged all over the toilets."

"Oh god …"

"Wait, it gets better. We have to leave so we go down to the train station and Hamish starts putting all sorts of shit into the ticket machine — New Zealand coins, peanuts — and breaks it so we have to walk to the next station."

"Is this true, Hamish?" she calls out.

"I don't know," I say, covering my head with a pillow.

"And the curator, Takumi, he's getting really stressed out by all of this and he says to me, 'Rapley san, is your friend insane?'" Rapley and Zlata both crack up laughing. "Eventually we're on the train and Hamish is passing out by this point, so I think the worst is over. But then after a few minutes he wakes up and starts singing this song about Moby Dick and eating whales. And these two fat businessmen opposite him start calling him names and telling him to shut up. And this fool gets up and is all like, 'What did you say to me?', like he's on K Road or some shit. And the businessman jumps up and they start wrestling with him. But he's so drunk he can't even hit them and all three of them fall over and start rolling around on the ground. At first I was going to jump in, but I was laughing so hard I couldn't breathe. It looked like he was being mauled by two emperor penguins ..."

I can hear Zlata laughing hysterically.

"... and when I pull them apart, no one's got so much as a scratch on them. Anyway, here's old drunky."

He throws the laptop back to me. Zlata's face is bright red and she's wiping tears out of her eyes.

"Well, I'm glad the trip wasn't a total waste, honey," she says.

16 ZLATA

IT WAS WHEN the single became a success that I decided to leave. Student radio picked it up first and then some commercial stations. In theory, this is what I had been working towards for over ten years. But, as usual, I'd been naïve.

I had wanted my music to leave my side and take thousands of lovers, imagining an audience gentle and discerning. Instead I found myself surrounded by skeletal faces smiling manically, their dead eyes following me down the street. When I played shows, people would yell tunelessly along to the words.

The video came out and it got worse. We filmed it in Sam's flat on Symonds Street. The idea was simple. Me, Sam and Louisa set up in the living room and mimed the song. We had earphones hidden from view, playing the track while the crowd danced to something much slower. Watching it reminded me of moving through the city that winter. The video didn't get much traction on television but it made it onto some music blogs and began getting thousands of hits on YouTube. Everything was coming together like a five-car pile-up.

* * *

We all met in front of the court. Apart from Louisa, who always had great style, everyone looked like they were in fancy dress. I had borrowed one of Bella's dresses that looked great on her, but she had deceptively large breasts and it hung around my body like a colourful sack. Sam looked like a pirate's secretary, with a white blouse with frills down the front and a black skirt. Freckles had on an ill-fitting grey suit making him look like the son of an eastern European used car salesman.

"Well, I hope his friends' lack of fashion sense isn't going to count against him," Louisa said as we headed up the escalator.

Nicholas met us inside, dressed like he was defending someone in the next case.

"Hey, guys," he said solemnly. We sat up the front of the courtroom.

"That's his mum," Freckles said, pointing to a large woman with messy white hair sitting alone and looking terrified. I got up and walked over to her.

"Hi, I'm a friend of Luke's."

She looked at me and said nothing.

"We're just sitting over there if you'd like to join us."

"Why would people your age want to hang out with my son?"

"I'm sorry for what happened." She pushed me and I stumbled back into a row of chairs.

"He wasn't like that before he met you people."

I turned and walked back to my seat.

"Don't worry, she's crazy," said Freckles.

But she was right.

* * *

They brought Luke out into the dock. He looked good in Nicholas's suit. It fitted him well. You could see that he would be handsome in a couple of years. He scanned the crowd and his face lit up when he saw us waving. Across the aisle was a large group of people watching Luke intently. They were obviously related, sharing the same beak-like nose and heavy frame. The court proceedings started and I was surprised to learn that the boy Luke had stabbed was only a year older than him. When they mentioned his name, Ben Talbit, a couple of the woman in the beak family started crying.

It was late afternoon when the court adjourned; no one said much when we went our separate ways. I was angry. Both you and Rapley should have been there. Though no one said as much, this was your fault. I ate takeaways in bed watching some awful TV series on my laptop, checking Skype whenever someone came online. I really needed to talk to you. But your icon remained red, and the next thing I knew my alarm was going off.

* * *

Back in the court room the angry little lawyer we hired for Luke did his best. He pleaded self-defence and talked of Luke's troubled upbringing and that he had recently started making music. But the prosecution lawyer was slow and considered. He painted a picture of Luke as a part of a violent gang of older criminals. He talked about how this gang had attacked Ben and his friends at a party a few weeks before the stabbing. How the knife Luke was carrying could only have been intended to seriously maim or kill. I watched Luke's face and wished the jury could have seen him before all of this; excited about life, kind and present. But all that had bled out when he stuck that knife in.

* * *

While the jury made up their mind about Luke's future, we drank coffee and tried to guess what other people in the waiting area were there for.

"Sex offender," Sam said about everyone.

Nicholas pointed to a man in a mismatched suit with pockmarks all over his face.

"Drugs, for sure."

* * *

The court made WINZ look like Rainbow's End. Hundreds of poor people waiting their turn to be humiliated. We got the word that a verdict had been reached and filed back into the court room. I sat down and saw that Luke's mother had been joined by two young women.

A jury member stood up to read the verdict. She looked like a school teacher I had when I was eight, not someone who would be passing judgement on someone's future.

"We find the defendant guilty of murder." Her words were clear and sharp, like the edge of a razor. I felt myself sink into my chair.

I looked at Luke and our eyes met. I wanted more than anything to run up and hug him, but he was already being led away.

* * *

Outside the court, everyone was crying. Louisa took the lead, ushering us into taxis to go back to hers and drink. I shared a cab with Nicholas. As we headed up Great North Road, I heard the opening chords of my song come on the radio.

"Can you let me out here," I said. The cab pulled over and I stumbled out and stood on the footpath.

15 HAMISH

WE'RE DRIVING BACK to Grey Lynn from the airport. The volcanoes surrounding the city rise up above the houses. After Tokyo, everything's in slow motion. Louisa just told us about Luke being found guilty. Everyone's quiet. I suddenly want to be a million miles from here.

A familiar sounding song comes on the radio.

"It's your song," yells Louisa.

"Oh god," says Zlata, leaning her head into the back of the front seat.

Rapley turns the radio up.

"It's Sam playing the drums."

"It sounds real professional."

"Here's the hook ..."

Lou is banging on the steering wheel along with the music.

"Everything happens for a stupid reason, everything happens for a stupid reason!" she yells.

I look over at Zlata. She's staring out the window. I take her hand. She squeezes back so tight it hurts.

* * *

"Yous want to come and drink some duty-free later?" I ask Louisa when we get to the house.

"I got the kids."

"Bring them down, or we could come up to yours."

"Okay, call me."

Inside, I lie on the bed and pull Zlata on top of me. She buries her face in my chest.

"You good?"

"Not really, honey. It's been a long month."

"How's Luke?"

"I don't know. His sentencing is in a few weeks. You should go see him."

"I will." The thought makes my stomach tight. Zlata pulls away from me.

"I have to go and do some interviews." She wipes her eyes on the sleeve of her hoodie.

"Are you crying?"

"It's good that you're back," she say, and leaves.

* * *

I'm on the deck smoking a joint when Sam turns up singing 'Big in Japan'.

"Heard you had a little adventure," she says, snatching the weed off me and having a toke.

"You know how it is."

"I know how you are, you fucking loser." She looks inside. "Is that big lummox here as well?"

"He's coming over soon with Nicholas and that."

"I wish Nicholas would stop not-fucking me."

"You want a vodka?" I say, heading inside.

"Yes I do, I'm big in Japan, I'm big in Japan."

"Have you been to see Luke?" I ask.

"Yeah."

"How is he?"

"He's in jail."

"I know, but is he okay?"

"No, he's in jail." I pass the vodka to Sam, who sculls it and hands it back.

"More please." I pour her another cup.

"I really think you and Rapley should go see him. I'm big in Japan, I'm big in Japan."

* * *

"Did you know Sam used to live in a halfway house?" Louisa asks. She's got one of the twins on her lap. The other kids are sleeping in Bella's room. We're in the living room, crowded round a small fan heater.

"That's not true," says Nicholas.

"It is. Tell him, Sam."

Sam readjusts her seat and starts telling the story, gesturing with her glass, spilling vodka on the carpet.

"It was when I was like 18 and I had to move back home because they cut off my dole. But I kept fighting with Mum and one day I came home and all my stuff was packed into rubbish bags out front of the house."

"Didn't you spray paint 'cunt' on her dog?"

"That's not the point. I was looking for somewhere to live and I was in Morningside and I saw a sign in the window of this house saying 'Room to let'. The house was falling to pieces so I was like, this has to be cheap. I ring up and it's like 70 bucks a week. So me and Lou go and get all the rubbish bags and I move in."

"That place was rank," Louisa says.

"Yeah, was pretty gross, just a mattress on the floor, mould everywhere, smelt like old dogs. I was drinking heaps then so it took me a couple of days to notice that everyone there was touched."

"Touched?" asks Nicholas.

"You know — special. Like one dude would stand out front of the house in his track pants listening to the horse races and singing Roy Orbison."

"I've seen that guy. You lived with him?"

"That's nothing. This other woman was deaf and she was always stealing my food. I put a lock on my door and kept the food in my room and she would break in through the window and eat it. She was like a hearing-impaired ninja. And then there was Jason."

"Oh yeah, he had Down syndrome, I think."

"I love Jason."

"Me too. He liked wearing women's clothes so we'd all dress up, put make-up on and go out. Man, that was the best."

"Remember how excited he got …"

"And there was this mean bitch, what was her name?"

"I can't remember."

"She was supposed to come and take care of them, but she only turned up every other day so I had to always be looking out for them."

"You didn't move out when you realised it was a halfway house?"

"No way, it was so cheap."

"You stayed there for like a year, right?"

"Yeah, I even made up my own sign language to talk to the deaf thief."

"We still hang with Jason sometimes."

"We should go see him soon."

* * *

I'm drunk by the time Zlata gets back; everything's soft and swaying. She leans in the doorway, playing with her hair.

"How was it?"

"Okay, just said the same thing over and over again."

"You must be used to that, living with Hammy," Sam says.

"When's the record out?" Nicholas asks. He's wearing these brown leather gloves and it's creeping me out.

"Next week," Zlata yawns.

"Wow, I'm excited."

"Hey, I'm going to go lie down. I got work tomorrow," Zlata says. "Night, everyone."

I start to follow her to the bedroom.

"Wait up," Rapley comes down the hall. We walk out onto the deck.

"Let's go see Luke tomorrow," he says. I hug myself against the cold.

"Can't tomorrow, got some shit on."

"Come on man, we have to go see him."

"Why's everyone telling me what to fucking do?"

"No one's telling you what to do."

"I don't want to go, okay?"

"We have to."

"I don't want to."

"Why not?"

"BECAUSE IT'S MY FAULT HE'S IN THERE."

The bedroom door opens and Zlata looks out.

"That's bullshit," says Rapley, walking back inside. Zlata looks at me then closes the door. I stand on the deck for a few minutes. I hate this shit: powerless, guilty, weak.

I kick a pot plant off the deck. It smashes on the footpath and I head off into the night.

14 ZLATA

OVER THE NEXT week you came up with one excuse after another for not visiting Luke. I gave up trying to reason with you. I was getting ready for the release and had to return to work after a couple of weeks off for recording and the court case. I was supporting both of us, as you were completely broke. You refused to even unpack the paintings that hadn't sold in Japan and your old habits of fleeing into the night had returned. We barely saw each other that week. On the Thursday I suggested we go to the park after work and talk. I could see you desperately trying to think of an excuse but in the end you agreed.

We sat on a patch of grass by the playground. I watched fat children in animal masks stumble around while their parents gazed into their phones. You kept fidgeting with a stick, breaking it into ever smaller sections.

"I'm going to leave after the album's done its thing," I said. You stopped playing with the stick and looked up at me in that way you always did when things were serious.

"Where?"

"I don't know, but I can't stay here." You started playing with the stick again. "I want you to come."

A child in a lion mask fell on the playground and started to cry. All the parents looked up at once. A woman went and retrieved it while the rest went back to their phones.

"I don't know," you said.

"Why? You want to stay here?"

"It's home."

"What is?" I could feel the blood rushing into my cheeks. "These streets filled with rich assholes? The flat you can't afford? The friends you constantly push away? The mother you never see? What part of this is home?"

"All of it," you said, getting up and tossing the pieces of stick away.

"You're stuck living in the past!" I shouted after you, making the parents look up briefly. "Everything's falling to pieces, or haven't you noticed?"

"So you want me to run way?"

You looked in pain. I shook my head.

"I'm trying, Zlata," you said eventually, "but you always want shit to be perfect." You stood there for a while longer.

"I don't fucking know what to do," you said quietly, before walking off.

I sat there watching you leave, then lay down on the grass and stared at the sky until my eyes hurt.

* * *

I had to work the day the album was released. I sat on the internet watching the praise flow in. It didn't feel like the person they were talking about was me or even that those songs were mine. The last six weeks had erased the woman who wrote them. I sat there, a stranger in my own life, an impostor who would be discovered any second. The label kept calling, no doubt wanting more of my time. I ignored them and chatted online to Alice about her children. She always had hilarious stories of their wild antics. I would have given anything to know the secret of her fire-proof optimism. At lunch I went and ate at the sushi shop across the road from the office. In the paper was a review of the album. They compared me to some American I'd never heard of and used words like 'quirky' and 'different', sealing it with four stars. I ate my avocado roll and looked at flights.

13 HAMISH

"YOU HAVE TO go to the seminar if you want to be eligible for the unemployment benefit."

"But I've been on it before."

"You still have to go to the seminar."

"When's the next one?"

"In a week."

I sigh, leaning back in my chair. The case manager's younger than me, her face fixed in a permanent frown. The heating's turned up too high and the place stinks like wet socks.

"Can I get a food grant?"

"Not unless you have a verified bank statement."

"I don't have that shit."

"Well, I can't give you a grant."

"But I've got no money."

"Do you want me to put you down for the seminar?"

"Nah, don't bother." I walk out into the freezing morning and head down Ponsonby Road.

I feel like an alien every time I come here these days. This place used to be sketchy, before money swept down and left wanky restaurants and fancy shoe stores in its wake. Back then our lives were filled with fear as well as boredom.

* * *

"Have you got a CV?" Nicholas asks. The shop's crowded, the windows all misted up.

"What would I put on it? Vandal and drug dealer?"

"I might be able to get you something washing dishes."

"Can't I cook?"

Nicholas laughs, "You're one of the worst cooks I know."

Someone does a fake cough. I turn round — there's a line of pissy rich people behind me.

"I've got to make some coffees. I'll ask the chef about the dishy job."

"Thanks, man."

I push past the customers, loudly saying 'Excuse me' every time I bump into someone, and wander towards the studio with my hood up. There's nothing as hopeless as being broke. Everyone gets a say in your life. You're not allowed secrets, you can't act on your impulses, you have to turn up where you're told, stand naked with your fucking hand out.

Rapley's up in the studio when I arrive, talking to some dark-haired girl with a knowing smile.

"Look who it is," he says. "This is Mel."

The girl gives me a wave.

"Where you been?" Rapley asks.

"Looking for work."

He starts laughing.

"Have you ever had a job before?"

"Yeah, I worked on that building site."

"For three days."

"Five."

The girl's still looking at me. She's pretty in a weird kinda way.

"I saw you on TV," she says.

"Really? Shit, I didn't think anyone saw that."

I go over to my corner, start throwing scraps of paper in the bin.

"I was talking to Linda, she said people are still keen to buy your shit. She was saying all the drama has given you a, what's the word?" He starts clicking his fingers, "mystique."

"Fuck that, man."

"What, you'd rather work minimum wage?"

"That art shit's not for me, man."

"What are you talking about? Your first show was a hit, you sold almost everything."

"It's bullshit, all that fucking watching what you say, people reading shit into everything."

"It's easy money, man."

"Yeah, so is dealing."

Rapley stands up. "Don't go back to that shit." There's a sadness in his voice that makes me even more angry.

"There you go, telling me what do."

"I'm just looking out for you, man."

"I never fucking asked you to."

I knock over a box of spray cans. They hit the ground and scatter over the floor. The girl jumps and moves back against the wall, that stupid smile still on her face like she's watching a movie. I storm down the stairs and out onto the street, bumping into some businessman.

"What!" I yell in his face. He throws his hands up and backs away.

* * *

Jamil's had his apartment for almost a year and still doesn't even own a fridge. There's a bed, a couple of couches and water damage down one of the walls. Apart from that, the shithole's empty. Skam opens the door and leads me into the living room with his swaying walk. Jamil's on one couch with two girls on either side of him. One's wearing a school uniform. Two other guys I've seen around are on the other couch staring at me. Skam goes and stands in the kitchen.

"What up, slut!" Jamil yells when I walk in the room. The girls laugh.

"Not much, man."

"Give him some room, girls." One gets up and sits on the arm of the couch. I take her seat.

"You want some shit?" he asks, holding up a glass pipe.

"Nah, I'm good."

"So when you going to do another show, cunt?"

"I'm not."

"But you were going to be my famous artist friend. I was going to use you to impress chicks." The girl in the school uniform takes the pipe off Jamil and starts to smoke from it.

"Greedy bitch," he says.

"Please tell me she's in fancy dress."

"Sophie, are you in fancy dress?"

"My name's Sasha," she says, breathing out the thick grey smoke.

"Like I fucking care."

The guys on the couch are still eyeballing me. Jamil puts his hand on the schoolgirl's thigh. I watch with a sick feeling in my gut as his fat fingers creep under her skirt.

"So, the little pussy went to jail?" Jamil says.

"Luke. You know his fucking name."

"Luke that killed that boy?" says the girl sitting next to me. "He was in my class."

"Fuck, he'll be getting it in there," Jamil says, removing his hand from the girl's crotch and taking the pipe back.

"What the fuck are you staring at?" I say to the two guys on the couch. They both jump and lower their eyes.

"Sorry bro, we just saw you on the TV."

12 ZLATA

MY PARENTS ALWAYS stressed the importance of working towards goals. Since they rarely agreed on anything, I took this to be good advice. They never told me the main purpose of a goal is distraction. I was addicted to living in those imagined futures, my aspirations keeping me from the here and now. Whenever a project was completed I threw myself into the next, terrified of what might grow in that void.

The album was something I'd worked towards most of my adult life. After its completion I wandered that empty space, my thoughts echoing around me. I began to second guess everything, unable to make new plans, wedged in limbo. The music had its own will and I was a passenger to its whimsical designs. You had become animal, something I coexisted alongside without means of communication, and it would be only a matter of time before I was fired from work.

Success reminded me of high school, looking up to a group of older kids. One day you finally make friends with them and realise they're as confused and frightened by life as you, just with nice shoes and pretty faces. I used to think that when journalists wrote about musicians they actually meant what they said, that their praise or condemnation was a product of passion. But they were just filling their word count. One of the interviewers was so woeful I had to suggest questions for her. Likewise, I had naïvely thought labels were at least interested in music. But they were populated by salesmen with expensive T-shirts who got free tickets to gigs. That shining prize was hollow to its core.

The single, 'Stupid Reason', went from strength to strength. The label pretended they'd never had any doubts. I went along with this charade – what else was there to do? The tour was fast approaching and I was afraid of how I would come out the other end. Louisa and Sam were going to play bass and drums. The fact that they were coming with me was the only thing that made the idea bearable.

I tried to visit Luke as much as possible, but it wasn't often. It didn't take long for that place to change him. His face became fat, he shaved his head and looked at least five years older. He spoke slowly now, with that distant air people adopt in such places. But he still held my hand the whole visit. The first couple of times he asked about you. I tried to make excuses, but I ended up saying I didn't know what you were doing. Luke told me some of Rapley's friends were looking out for him and that things weren't so bad. When he spoke like this, I smiled and nodded. I liked to pretend that somehow things would work out for all of us. It was only fair.

* * *

"I warned you about that lifestyle," my mother said, the shitty reception making her sound so distant.

"I know. I just thought I would have more control."

"You never do though, honey. You'll drive yourself mad expecting it."

"How did you handle it?"

"I didn't. I drank and did drugs and then I met your father and quit."

"I'm thinking of leaving when this is done."

"You do what you have to. I know you'll sort things out."

"I think I might go by myself."

"Things not working out with Hayden?"

"Hamish. No, I feel like I have to keep holding things together."

"Don't let a man take your light from you."

"I need something else to work towards, I think."

"Just enjoy what's happening now, because it'll be over soon."

* * *

The night before the album launch I bought a bottle of wine and went round to Hayley's. I'd had a call from Rapley earlier in the day, saying Luke had been sentenced. He received fifteen years in the end. The phone suddenly became very heavy and I let it fall from my hand. When I told you, you sat on the couch staring at the same piece of carpet for hours, while I busied myself answering emails and restringing my guitar, trying not to think of what Luke would be going through. Me and Hayley had barely seen each other since the exhibition, but I was running late and by the time I arrived she'd already left for work. I found

Christina lying on a couch, listening to what sounded like a fridge motor amplified. She was off hard drugs and had gone back to uni.

"Hey, Z," she said, turning the music down when I walked in. "What do you think of this new song I found?"

We sat on the balcony and talked and drank. She told me about turning her life around.

"I have so much time now I'm relatively sober, like I had even more time before, of course, because I wasn't sleeping, but it was a haze. Now it's like, what the fuck am I supposed to do all day? What do normal people do?"

"Work and watch TV, I guess."

"God, if there's anything worse than full-time work I don't want to know about it."

"I feel the same with this whole music lark. Like if I play my cards right I could make some kind of living, but it just feels empty."

"Falling isn't so far from flying," said Christina.

"A toast to the virtues of failure," I cried.

We clinked glasses, laughing.

11 HAMISH

THE WINDSCREENS OF the parked cars are white. Hank Williams plays in my headphones. I walk fast, my backpack rattling. A car drives past, slowing down. We exchange glances, then both look away. I don't pass anyone going down Mountain View road. My mind feels clear; I'm not thinking about Luke or Zlata, or being broke. I find it calming out here, among the night. Like a surfer out beyond the breakers. No one can reach me, apart from the sharks. But I can run fast. Back on land, everything's fucked. I haven't seen Rapley in days, Zlata looks like death, Luke probably won't talk to me even if I do go see him. And what would I say if I did? I've protected that kid for years. Had his back, given him money and clothes, fed him and now I'm fucking useless. But all that's behind me. I pull out a pen and hit up a lamp post, my hand dancing across the metal in one fluid movement.

I'm at the wall. I check if anyone's around. No one to spot for me tonight. I like it that way sometimes.

"She's long gone and I'm lonesome blue," sings Hank. I get the outline done when I notice someone's parked at the other end of the street. I stuff my cans into my backpack and start walking quickly towards the main road. I can hear the car following me. I get around the corner and sprint up past the dairy on New North Road and jump the fence, through a backyard and come out onto the back of the tracks. I jump another fence and wait and listen. If it's the cops, they'll bring the dogs out, in which case I'm fucked. I hear nothing apart from my ragged breathing. I put my headphones back in and listen to Hank while I catch my breath.

I start thinking about Zlata, missing her and angry at the same time. She always wants the best of both worlds, feeding off everyone's craziness, their stupid stories and fucked-up lives, then pulling away and calling us psychos when shit goes down. As if the two aren't related.

It's hard sometimes to explain things to her, things which aren't spoken about in the group, things we all try our best to never think of. Like this shit with Luke. I mean, she thinks she understands, but her life's so different — safe, warm, a brother and parents who love her, travelling, an education, the whole fucking dream. And that's fine. Honestly, I'd swap with her in a second, but the past is like a shitty tattoo. Once you've got it, you have to wear it.

I guess I thought maybe she'd lift me up into her life. Instead it feels like I've dragged her down into mine.

I snap out of it, find myself walking down the tracks. This was a tradition when we were young. We'd steal bread from the Tip-Top factory and do tags beneath this overpass that everyone called Combat Zone. Now the bread factory's burnt down and the walls beneath the underpass are painted a shitty green. Below me on the motorway a car pulls around but doesn't slow. I remember how jumpy I was coming down here with Rapley when I was young. Most of the older crews were more proficient in violence than graffiti. It didn't help that Rapley never backed down to anyone. Many times we walked home with black eyes and blood noses 'cos someone said something about our school or accused us of some bullshit.

"Why did we have to fight those guys?"

"Cos they said Springs sucks."

"It does — you hate school."

"It's not the point, bro."

Our friend's mother used to sell weed near here. We'd hang out and get high. Some of her customers were older writers and rappers. We'd always try to hang with them, but usually we got too high and ended up making fools of ourselves. It was a fun time though. Learning different techniques, making friends and enemies every weekend, finding something that was worth getting a black eye for. This was all before the internet; back then all we had was the odd graffiti mag that got handed around and the older heads. But all times seem simpler when you look back on them, I guess.

10 ZLATA

A LL I COULD see was light. My left hand made
chords while the right one strummed. I looked
behind me. Sam was smashing away on the drums, her
skinny limbs flailing in every direction. To my left, Louisa
was playing bass, calm, staring down the audience. I turned
around and started to sing. Every so often people burst
through the wall of light and landed by my feet. I watched
one of my beers fly off and empty out onto the carpet.
Nicholas was near the front, singing along. The song ended
and everyone cheered.

"Thanks," I mumbled into the mic, trying to find
another drink.

"This next song is what you're all here for." I motion to
Sam and she counts us in. As soon as I hit the first chord
everyone lets out a roar.

We fly through the first verse. Sam is playing too fast
but it adds to the excitement. When we reach the chorus,
the whole venue explodes.

"Everything happens for a stupid reason," everyone's yelling along with me. A couple fall onto the stage and start clawing at the mic stand. I put my foot on the base to keep it from falling over. Sam keeps speeding up; I struggle to get the words out in the next verse. Not that anyone seemed to notice. Things were falling apart by the time we reached the last chorus, bodies covered the stage, broken glass and beer everywhere.

"Everything happens for a stupid reason, everything happens for a stupid reason." I struck the last chord and stood there, looking for you.

* * *

At the merch table I tried to get people to buy CDs. I felt stupid hawking my obsolete wares. Sam came stumbling out, holding two longnecks.

"Good show," she says with a mocking tone. "Great show, good set, that was choice." She skulls out of one of the bottles. "Your fans are sycophants," she adds, sitting next to me.

"They're just being friendly."

We're both still sweating, our faces flushed.

"I have too many fucking friends." She finishes one of the bottles and throws it behind her.

"You're so rambunctious when you drink."

"Don't call me names, bitch," Sam says. "Especially ones I don't understand."

Louisa came out looking fresh in a new outfit.

"Look at you," I said.

"You trying to get laid tonight?"

"God, you'd think it was a crime to look good with you two."

"What you talking about?" Sam asked, climbing on her chair. "I look like a million dollars." She held out her faded Patti Smith T-shirt drenched in sweat.

A guy with a thick head of curly black hair edged towards the desk.

"Umm, hey, really liked the set," he said to me.

"Did you?" Sam asks, leaping off the seat and landing next to him. "Did you like the set?"

"Ahh, yeah." The guy looked at all three of us as if he'd made a fatal error.

"Thanks, I'm glad you ..." I started to say.

"Did you really like it though?" Sam said, "I mean, really and truly love it?"

The guy backed away and left.

"Fuck, Sam, I could have sold him a CD."

"That loser didn't have any money."

In the end, I managed to sell ten albums. Five years ago it would have been considered a failure, but things had changed. Me and Louisa shared a cab home.

"Where's Hammy?" she asked.

"I don't know. Probably painting on a fence."

"Things not good with you guys?"

"Since Luke and Japan he's been a real dick." The cab sped down Newton Gully, spraying rainwater in its wake. The city lights flared against the window.

"He's like that, he can't handle stress. I'm not making excuses for him."

"The tour's next week."

"I know, I'm excited."

"Yeah," I say watching the meter tick over.

* * *

When I got home you were in the lounge watching fighting on the television. The room was filled with smoke.

"Hey."

"Hey." I sat down next to you.

"How was the show?" you said, not facing me, your eyes half-closed.

"Why didn't you come?"

"I was painting."

I sat staring at you until you turned around.

"Why didn't you come?" I repeated. You looked away and then turned back again.

"I don't know. I didn't want to see everyone."

"You could have said."

"I know."

"Is this it? Is this how we're going to end this?"

You looked at me wide-eyed as though I'd just punched you again.

"No." You took my hand. "Things are just fucked up at the moment."

"When are they ever not?"

"I know but come on, look at what's happened the last month."

"It's the same for everyone."

"Yeah, but like, people blame me and …" You let go of my hand and stared at the TV, where some steroid-addled brute was beating another man to a pulp.

"And what?" You said nothing. "That's just what this fucking city is like; that's why I'm leaving." You gave me that look again and despite myself I stroked your face.

"You can come," I said, my voice softening.

"Yeah." You turned back to the violence on the television.

* * *

That night we fucked for the first time in weeks. It started out slow. We kissed for a long time, your hands moving over me. I climbed on top of you and we fucked slow, still kissing.

"I missed you," I whispered. "I missed this."

You said nothing, just stared into me. But then the mood changed. You were on top of me holding me down with a fistful of my hair. Fucking me hard, your face tense.

"Fuck you," I hissed while you thrust into me. You let go of my hair and pressed your hand over my mouth. I bit it as hard as I could when I started to come.

After you came, you fell down next to me like you'd been shot.

You started to snore and I lay there feeling the last of you run out of me.

9 HAMISH

THIS REALLY SUCKS. The hot water's run out. A pile of dishes towers over me. The chef keeps yelling to get shit out of the fridge. Most of the time I've got no idea what he's on about. I'm dripping sweat and wipe my face on my tea towel.

"What the fuck are you doing? That's for the dishes, not your face!"

I take a deep breath and go back to scrubbing the pots in cold water. Nicholas runs in.

"We need more coffee!"

"Where is it?"

"In the storeroom!"

He dashes back out front. I start searching for the coffee, but can't see it anywhere.

"I can't find the coffee," I say to the chef, who's tossing ingredients into four different pans.

"What the fuck do you want me to do about it?" he yells.

I go back to the storeroom and search again.

"I need some fucking onions cut now!"

I still can't find the coffee. I come out and start cutting onions.

"Where's the coffee?" Nicholas says, running back out.

"I couldn't find it."

"Fuck!" he shouts and sprints out the back.

"Where's those onions?"

* * *

I smell like rotten vegetables. Everything hurts as I lie in bed: feet, legs back, head.

Zlata's stuffing clothes into a duffel bag.

"How was work?" she asks.

"So fucked."

"It can't have been that bad."

"Was all I could do not to knock out the chef!"

"Don't do that, punching your boss is frowned upon." She looks up and smiles for the first time in ages.

I laugh.

"I'll try not to."

"How many pairs of socks do I need for two weeks?"

"Just take all of them."

"I have a lot of socks," she says. "Should I take something nice to wear in case?"

"I guess."

"What if we get invited to a fancy-pants dinner or something?"

"I don't think they have fancy dinners in the South Island."

"You never know."

"Take one then."

She stuffs more clothes in her bag, then comes and lies next to me.

"Are you going to be okay when I'm gone?"

"Sure."

"Really? I don't want to worry about you."

"Don't worry. I'm going to work and save."

She kisses me.

"I'm scared," she says.

"It'll be okay," I hold her, staring at the mould on the ceiling.

* * *

I'm up at 6 a.m. to go to work. Zlata's still sleeping.

"I'm off, baby." I kiss her cheek.

"I'm going to come see you on your break," she mumbles, her eyes closed.

* * *

It's dark outside. I walk fast to warm up. Can't remember the last time I woke up this early. The kitchen's warm at least. The chef's quiet while we prep. I put on some music. After half a song he pulls it out, puts on some R'n'B bullshit.

"I can't stand country music," he says.

Nick comes out back and hands me a coffee.

"Careful, it's strong."

By the breakfast rush, my hands are shaking.

"Eggs!" the chef yells.

I go to the fridge and pass 'em out.

"No, the cooked ones," he says, thrusting them back at me. I start going through the packed fridge till I find them in a white bucket of water. I go back to making sandwiches for the counter.

"Bacon!" he yells.

"What?"

"Pass the fucking bacon."

I get the bacon out.

"And put the eggs away."

* * *

Zlata turns up at 2 p.m. We sit out front and share a juice.

"Is it better today?" she asks.

"Yeah, nah," I say, glaring at the chef, "I hate this shit."

"Everyone hates their job."

"True."

"I don't know why you don't make some more art."

"Nah."

"Things go wrong sometimes — doesn't mean you should give up."

She's right, but still, I can't handle the idea of my shit being picked over again, being judged by assholes. I've been thinking the first show was just a fluke.

"I don't know."

Louisa pulls up in her car with Sam beeping the horn.

"Get in bitch, we're taking this car to Invercargill!" Sam yells.

Zlata hugs me. I don't want to let her go.

"Be careful," she says.

"What do you mean?" But I know exactly what she's talking about.

"I don't know. Love you."

"Same." She pulls herself slowly away from me and gets in the car, waving as they drive away.

8 ZLATA

WE PULLED OUT of the city's grasp and sped along the motorway. We'd decided to drive the length of the country and stay on people's floors to save as much money as possible. Louisa drove erratically, braking suddenly for no apparent reason and then speeding off again. Sam was playing Melissa Etheridge on the stereo.

"Please turn that shit off," Louisa begged.

"Don't be so homophobic," Sam replied, turning it up.

I shoved one of the backpacks onto the floor, stretched out and listened to Jonathan Richman on my headphones.

Watching the sky race past, I was with Luke in his cell. Day after empty day, with only his meals to break things up. It was like a 15-year flight to a hostile future. When I was young, we used to ask each other, do you think you could ever kill someone? Of course I said no; I felt guilty hitting my mother's dog after it pissed on my bed. But seeing what happened to Luke made me realise how easy it would be. Some booze mixed with adrenalin and a dumb situation, and the next thing you know your youth is taken from you.

I had visited him just before we left and talked about the album and the release party. He smiled and nodded, even laughed a couple of times.

"Thanks," he said, when I hugged him goodbye, "for being so kind."

* * *

We pulled into a gas station in the middle of nowhere.

"I need to piss, I need to piss!" Sam yelled, running inside.

Lou got out and stretched, then leaned back into the car.

"You want anything?"

"See if they've got any chips without animals in them."

I sat up. All around us were fields speckled with the occasional sheep. In the distance a mountain rose up half-covered in trees, the other half stripped bare. I got out and took a deep breath. Despite the smell of gasoline, the air was fresh.

"Someone's written their name in shit on the toilet wall," Sam said, walking back to the car.

"Is their name Sam?"

"Ha ha."

"Can you eat Pringles?" Lou called from the door of the gas station.

"If they're plain ones."

"God, you're difficult," Sam said.

I picked up my water bottle and chased her around the car.

The first show was in Hamilton. We drove down the main street slowly, looking for the venue. Everyone we passed stopped and stared at us. Someone yelled something at us from the footpath.

"I fucking hate this place," said Sam.

"Don't worry, we'll play and drive to Wellington tonight," said Lou.

"You sure?"

"You want to stay here any longer than you have to?"

The venue was a concrete box at the bottom of a flight of stairs. We sound checked for over an hour but couldn't get anything close to a good sound.

"That's as good as it's going to get," the sound man said limping off.

Lou looked at me. I shrugged.

"I guess if he's given up, that's that."

"Let's eat something then," Sam said, throwing her sticks on the ground.

I went up to the girl behind the bar.

"Do you know if there's any vegetarian places to eat round here?" I asked.

"What?"

"Places that have vegetarian food ..."

She stared at me and walked off.

* * *

The support band played the kind of weird punk/funk fusion that comes from existing in a cultural vacuum. They weren't very good, but made up for it with youthful enthusiasm. By the time we took the stage, the place was packed.

"Anyone got any lollies?" Sam kept yelling into the snare mic.

I hit a chord and let my guitar feed back. Louisa came in underneath, playing a roaming bass line. Sam was so busy yelling shit that she missed her cue and we had to do the whole cycle again. The second time around the drums came crashing in and everyone started leaping up and down. The set went quickly. Sam managed to keep the tempo this time and we played heaps better than in Auckland. The crowd kept asking for more even after we did the encore numbers. We ended up playing a couple of Fuck Yous songs with me trying to keep up on the bass.

* * *

"How many CDs did you sell?" Sam asked.

The headlights cut into the night.

"Three."

"And my mother told me there's no future in music."

* * *

I was in the passenger seat. The heater pumped hot air onto my feet. The night was thicker out here. I thought how you would love it. Staring at the open road ahead of us, I felt free for the first time in weeks. Then my mind travelled back to Luke's cell. If things had been different, he would've probably been with us, him and Sam arguing, making us laugh with his inane freestyles.

"Well, we played better tonight," Louisa said, pulling me out of my thoughts.

"Yeah, it was pretty tight."

"Looks like we should learn some more of your old songs for encores," she said to Sam, taking a late turn that made me grab the door handle. "In the South Island they always want you to play forever."

"Those hicks like to get their money's worth," Sam said, leaning into the front. "Can you put Melissa back on?"

"I don't think that's going to happen, dear," said Lou, pushing Sam into the back seat by her face. Then she pressed down on the accelerator and we sped deeper into the night.

* * *

I woke up the next morning on somebody's floor, Sam curled by my feet. Pulling on my jeans, I walked outside and stood on the road in bare feet, looking out over Wellington city. We were in Aro Valley, on a steep hill surrounded by houses perched among trees. At the bottom the city began, a few handfuls of grey buildings that led to the harbour. I went back inside and bumped into a tall, half-naked man with a giant black beard.

"Hey, I think I slept on your floor."

"You're Zlata," he said smiling, a large wound of white teeth opening up in the thick hair. "I saw your video."

"Oh, cool."

"I'm Joshua."

I shook his hand.

"So you're the brains of this operation?" he said, walking into the kitchen.

"Hardly, I'm just dragging these two round the country, trying to sell CDs for the label."

"You want coffee?" he asked.

"Oh, yes please." He reached up and grabbed two cups. He had a long scar across his lean torso.

Just then, Louisa walked out wearing a guy's T-shirt.

"Are you making coffee?" she asked, her voice croaky.

"Sure am."

She kissed Joshua and sat down at the table. "I'm so fucking tired," she groaned, putting her head in her hands.

"You should sleep more."

"I can't, I'm used to the children waking me up."

"I was about to say to Zlata we should head into town soon."

Louisa shook her head. "Whatever you do, don't wake Sam up. She's unbearable when she's tired."

* * *

It was a cold day. The four of us walked down Cuba Street. Joshua had to stop every few minutes to greet people he knew — a motley crew of hippies, skaters and punks. Every time he mentioned the show, most people said they were already coming.

"Should be packed tonight," he said.

We headed down to the bucket fountain. Joshua had said he'd get Sam some weed. We sat and watched people strolling past, most of them smiling and laughing despite the cold. The label rep rang and told me I had an interview on the radio at 6pm.

A small weasel with a filthy hoodie came up and sat with us.

"Hey, guys," he said in a whiny voice.

"How much you want?" Josh asked Sam.

"Can you do a hundy bag?"

The weasel nodded and pulled out a bag of weed and handed it to Sam. She looked over at Louisa.

"What, you want me to pay for your drugs?"

"Come on, I'll pay you back."

"Fuck," she said, going into her purse and handing the money to the weasel.

"Chur chur," he said, and slipped away.

* * *

The studio was a tiny box sitting six storeys up. Windows looked out over the city. In the foyer, a group of people were drinking beer. The DJ obviously didn't know who I was.

"So, how long have you guys been a band?" he asked absent-mindedly, while cuing up the next song.

"Is that your lead question?" Sam said. "She's the band. Read that bit of paper in front of you; it's called a bio." The DJ looked up, with small angry eyes.

"Sorry," I said, pulling the mic away from Sam. "Well, I've been making music for years, but this is my first proper album."

"And what can people expect from tonight's show?" Sam swung the mic back over to her.

"Really? Well, I don't know, maybe a lecture on Eastern philosophy pertaining to ... oh, that's right, we make music."

"Stop being an asshole," I said.

"Oh, this guy is the worst."

"So, it doesn't mean ..." Louisa stepped forward and pushed Sam out of the way.

"Yeah, it's going to be great. You should all come down, it's only $10 and we're on at 11pm." The DJ stared at us, confused.

"Dead air, honey," Louisa said, leaning into the mic. The DJ pressed play and the first bars of 'Stupid Reason' filled the studio.

* * *

We ended up in the bathroom doing lines off the toilet seat.

"Fuck, this is classy," Sam said, sniffing, her eyes watering.

"What is this?"

"Either coke, speed, MDMA or K," Sam said, handing me a rolled up note. "Hopefully not K 'cos then we're not playing tonight."

I did the line, my nose burnt and the chemical taste dripped down the back of my throat.

"Jesus, that's harsh."

Louisa patted me on the back.

"You'll be okay." She took the note from me and quickly did her line.

"Okay, should we go and entertain everyone?" she asked, pocketing the money.

We stepped out and started pushing through the crowd. The place was packed; I had never played in front of that many people before. We got on stage and I felt the drugs kicking in. My head was light and I was smiling so hard my cheeks hurt. I picked up my guitar and turned on the amp. Sam did a quick fill and Louisa checked her bass.

"Ready?"

"Yeah, bitch!" Sam yelled.

I turned around and stared into 600-odd eyes all looking at us expectantly. I let the first chord ring out while the bass came in underneath. This time Sam got her cue and we kicked into the song. I closed my eyes and began to sing. The song was about losing your mind every night only to find yourself sane in the morning.

It ended and I opened my eyes and looked out over the cheering crowd. Streaks of colour followed my eyes. We played the single early in the set that night. I wanted it to be out of the way so we could concentrate on other songs. Lou was worried everyone would lose interest afterwards, but we held the crowd until the last note rang out. Afterwards we had a lock-in at the bar and drank and danced until being shoved out at dawn.

* * *

We spent a few more days in Wellington. The next gig wasn't till the following Thursday. Louisa was with Joshua most of the time, while me and Sam smoked weed and wandered through the city.

"I talked to Rapley this morning. He said Luke seems heaps better," Sam said as we walked up towards Newtown.

"Really? God, I hope so."

"You reckon you could live here?" She asked.

"I don't think so. I want to go somewhere smaller."

"Smaller than this?"

"Yeah, get away from everything."

"You think too much."

"Probably. How about you?"

"Live here? Nah, too many fucking hippies."

* * *

On Thursday morning we drove onto the Interislander ferry. It was a sunny day so we sat on deck as the boat pulled into Cook Strait. Sam rabbited on about how much she hated the South Island. Louisa was unusually quiet. When Sam went to the bar to get beers I asked if she was okay.

"Yeah, I just quite like Joshua."

"He seems cool."

"He is, but he lives down here so, you know," she said, smiling sadly. I put my arm round her and watched Wellington disappear as we headed into open waters.

* * *

The ferry pulled into the Marlborough Sounds, and hills covered in thick forest rose out of the water. The odd house looked out curiously towards the passing ship. A few small boats were anchored off the shore.

"Look at that," I said. "I'd love to live somewhere like this."

Both Lou and Sam looked at me with smirks on their faces.

"You'd go insane," said Lou.

"What the fuck would you do all day?"

"I don't know; make music, hang out with Hammy." They both started laughing.

"I'm sorry," Louisa said. "But if you think Hamish would be able to live somewhere like that, you're nuts."

* * *

The Nelson gig was a complete disaster. Everyone had said to avoid the place but the label insisted. Ten people showed up and three of them left halfway through the set. Sam ended up stabbing her stick through the snare drum so we wouldn't have to keep playing.

Afterwards we drank with the five members of the audience who stuck around. Sam hooked up with a guy with massive arms who looked 18. He and his friends took us to a bar they said was the best in Nelson. It turned out to be a strip club. Me and Louisa sat nursing our beers while bored naked woman danced out of time to dated pop songs.

"Well, I'm glad we added this stop to the tour," Louisa said, while Sam dry humped the 18-year-old next to us.

* * *

Sam had promised she would meet us at the hostel at 10 a.m.

Of course she didn't show, and her phone was turned off. After an hour, we decided to drive up and down the main street and eventually spotted her coming out of McDonald's with the 18-year-old.

"What the fuck!" Louisa yelled, pulling the car up next to her. The 18-year-old stood back, looking sheepish.

"I'm just getting some food."

"You know that we've got to drive to Christchurch."

"Yeah, so?" Sam said, chewing on her burger.

"Get in the car."

"See you," she said to the 18-year-old, and hopped in. We pulled off, leaving the poor kid looking shocked, holding his hamburger.

* * *

We drove down State Highway 6. I sat in the front with the window down, feeling the wind on my face. Sam kept passing me joints while we listened to *The Boy with the Arab Strap*. At Hanmer Springs we went to the hot pools. Me and Sam were so stoned Louisa had to pay and usher us towards the pools.

"Fuck, you two are useless," she laughed.

"He wasn't 18, by the way."

"He was, he was an 18-year-old forestry worker."

"He was 20 and he worked at the fish place."

"And you left him outside McDonald's? Are you crazy?"

"Fuck you."

"Poor guy," I said, "The look on his face when you jumped in the car."

"He was shit in bed. Lucky I even let him buy me McDonald's."

* * *

In a rest stop we ate chips and salad sandwiches Louisa had made at the hostel. Cars screamed past, racing towards the next chapter of their lives. The open road used to scare me almost as much as the ocean. I texted you about Nelson and that I missed you.

"Where are we staying, again?" I asked Louisa.

"With Sam's friend Nick."

"Fuck, I better tell him we're coming." Sam pulled out her phone.

"You haven't told him yet?"

"Yeah, nah, it's sweet."

"The one thing we got you to organise."

"Chill out, dick. Nick, how are you?" she said holding her hand up in Louisa's face.

"Yeah, well I'm actually going to be in Christchurch in an hour ..."

"... Yeah ..."

"... I know."

"Can me and my friends stay with you?"

"Three ..."

"Choice ..."

"See you soon!"

She hung up and gave Louisa a smug look.

* * *

When we first entered Christchurch we drove through tree-lined suburbs. It was hard to see any real effects of the earthquake. Sam kept flicking through the radio stations.

"They must be playing your song on here somewhere."

Drawing closer to the centre, we passed a few damaged buildings. Then rounding a corner we got a view of the city for the first time. Louisa pulled the car over.

"What the fuck," said Sam. The end of the street was barricaded off. Beyond it, the ruins of the city sat huddled. A few people in high-vis vests wandered the streets. Some buildings were gone altogether, others stood with their innards exposed.

"I guess you can't go this way any more," Louisa said, pulling a U-turn.

* * *

"Come see the cup," Nick said, leading us outside. We followed him out of his apartment into a small concrete yard.

"See, it survived the quake." He pointed to a teacup balanced on the fence, adjusted his cap and walked back inside.

"What a crazy fucking thing," Sam said, following him. "I was worried about you when I heard."

"You can't have been that worried. After the quake, I only got three texts and one was from the video shop saying I had late fees."

We sat in his lounge, smoking weed and listening to Nick and Sam swap ridiculous stories.

"You remember 9/11?" Nick asks.

"Of course I fucking do."

"Well, you know Harley?"

"The writer?"

"Yeah, we were all at my place in the morning. You know, when we lived above the fish mart. We got a text from my sister saying turn on the TV. So we're watching the news and everyone's freaking out, or saying good job, ya know. But Harley was being all quiet ... contemplative or whatever."

"Don't use dictionary words."

"Thinking, you dunce. Anyway he suddenly disappears. No one really thinks much of it, we keep watching the footage on the news and getting blazed. Then late at night he comes back with all this shit: Moët, new shoes, a watch, this big wheel of cheese. While everyone in the shops is losing their minds, fixated on the television, Harley snuck in and racked shit!"

"Fuck, that's classic."

"This other time he was stealing paint and the shopkeeper tries to stop him. So Harley clocks him with his skateboard and runs out. But he runs straight into an undercover cop and gets arrested. He's in the cells until the next day when he's got court. But he's a vegetarian and all they give him to eat is McDonald's."

"He wouldn't eat it?"

"Nah, he's morally opposed to that kind of thing. Anyway he goes to court in the morning and his last name starts with a W so he's not getting called for ages, and he's real hungry but he's broke. So he goes up to the dairy by the court and racks some instant noodles but there's a couple of cops in the diary and they snap him and he gets arrested again."

"You're shitting me."

"It's true."

"What was he going to do with instant noodles in court?"

"Fuck knows."

* * *

After soundcheck we picked up Nick's friend Jay. Sam had played me his music before. I liked his pleading, melancholy rap songs, and he had a haunting, ethereal voice. It was hard to put that sound to the lanky guy sitting next to me, wearing a panda hat.

"Hey, Nick," he said nervously, "can we get some lollies?"

"That's what I'm talking about," said Sam. For the next hour we drove around what was left of the city, stopping at various dairies to pick up particular treats.

"You can't find this anywhere else in Christchurch," Jay said defensively, getting back in the car with a can of Dr Pepper.

"We need to get dinner; we got to play soon."

"We'll go to the KFC," said Nick.

"Zlata's vego," said Lou.

"Not you too. You can just have some chips," he said, pulling into the drive-thru.

* * *

After the show it took Nick three tries to get the keys in the ignition.

"Don't tell me you're drunk," Louisa said.

"Okay, then," he slurred, starting the car.

We all went back to his place and drank and smoked weed. I talked to Jay about music for a while. The whole time he played some game on his phone.

"I'm not doing music any more."

"Why not?"

"Just don't want to." He leaned so far back in his chair he was almost lying down.

Suddenly the house started shaking. At first I thought it was a truck driving past.

"The fuck!" Sam said, dropping her beer. I grabbed Jay's arm. The shaking stopped and they laughed at us.

"That happens every other day," said Nick, getting Sam another beer.

"How can you live like this?"

"Where we going to go?" Jay said, briefly looking up from his phone.

* * *

Jay and Nick tagged along for our show in Dunedin. Before we left, Jay gave us methadone pills. Louisa sat slumped in her seat, driving so slowly we were constantly being overtaken by irate drivers, horns blaring.

"I think we should speed up," Sam mumbled.

"Okay." Lou put her foot down, making the car go marginally faster.

* * *

We stopped by a river and Louisa and Sam both puked behind a dead tree.

"I should have told you guys they were quite strong," Jay said, leaning on a picnic table, playing on his phone.

"You got any more Dr Pepper?" Nick asked. Jay fished one out of his backpack and threw it to him.

Sam came out from behind the tree, spitting and wiping her face with her T-shirt.

"Fuck you," she said, walking past Jay. She snatched the soft drink out of Nick's hand, swirled some of it round in her mouth and spat it out.

* * *

"I can't find this place on my phone," Jay said. We stood around the car in the centre of Dunedin, looking for the venue.

"It's called Chick's Hotel."

"Yeah, but it's not in the city." He studied his phone again. "Hold on, it's way out in Port Chalmers."

"What the fuck?"

"You mean we're not even playing in Dunedin?" Sam asked.

We followed a thin road out along the coast. Beneath the sullen sky, green hills stretched to the horizon; beside the road, the ocean bubbled away. We saw nobody the entire drive. The odd house stood watchful on the hillside, its windows dark. If Christchurch was what cities would look like after the apocalypse, then this was the rural version.

The hotel was in a fishing village. Inside it was dark and homely. The owner greeted us and gave us a quick tour. There was a small stage in a room the size of someone's lounge. A ping pong table sat behind it. We were led up stairs to where we would be staying.

"Someone got killed up here," Jay mumbled. "I saw it on TV."

* * *

I did the door that night. It was considered the worst job, but I didn't mind it. You got to meet people and get a gauge of the audience. That night it was more varied than usual: students from the city, a few fishermen, some tourists and a couple of drunk regulars. We didn't have a support act, but we managed to convince Jay to get up and do some songs while Sam and Lou played behind him. He got on stage and looked so shy I almost couldn't watch. But the minute he started rapping a change came over him. His words flowed perfectly over the drums. Even when Sam lost the beat at one point he slowed down and sped up to match her. He glided around the stage, his body movements accentuating his words. After four songs he got off stage and instantly shrank back into himself, but this time wearing a smile.

Although there can't have been more than 40 people in the crowd, this was the best show I ever did. We played fast and tight, the songs asked no questions. We didn't bother trying to win anyone over. Instead we threw everything we had at them. By the time we closed the set with 'Stupid Reason' I was soaked with sweat. I thanked everyone and started what would be the last song I would ever play as Picnic.

After the show, we drank into the night. First with the locals and then, after they left, with the owner. He wore an old black suit that looked like it had seen the wrong side of a few too many nights. We swapped stories of our dreams and travels while Sam played table tennis with Jay.

Eventually we drank ourselves sober and retreated upstairs to bed. The next morning I woke up in pain. I went downstairs to try to find some water. When I got back to the room, my phone was ringing.

7 HAMISH

I WAS UP painting till three in the morning. The cops came, I had to jump a fence and twisted my ankle. Now I'm at work. I keep drinking coffee to stay awake. We got slammed in the morning, using up most of the lunch prep. Now I'm chopping vegetables while the dishes pile up behind me.

"Did you batter that chicken?" the chef calls over his shoulder.

"Not yet, I will after the onions."

He mutters something and keeps cooking. I pour the chopping board of onions into the 40-litre bucket and limp over to the cool room. Check my phone, but there's nothing from Zlata.

"The chicken!" yells the chef.

* * *

I went to see Rapley last night at the studio. We hadn't spoken for a couple of weeks and I knew he was pissed at me. I decided to try and make things right. He was drinking beers with Nicholas and Freckles when I turned up.

"'Sup guys?" I said, standing by the door. Everyone gave me the evils. Freckles put his beer down and pushed past, out the room.

"What's up with him?"

"What do you think?" Rapley said.

I walked over to the table.

"Look, I'm sorry 'bout being a dick and everything. I was just real upset, you know."

Rapley stood there, staring at me.

"Say something," I said, my voice breaking slightly.

"I said a lot of things and you kept telling me you didn't want to hear them."

"I know but, shit's fucked up."

"We all love Luke, we all got shit going on. You think I want to be carrying you my whole life, man?"

"I know, but …"

"It's like you think whatever happens to you is the main event in everyone's lives. I got my own fucking problems."

I stood there. I didn't know what to say.

"Have you been to see him?"

"No," I say, looking at a splatter of red paint on the ground.

Rapley shook his head. "Just get out, okay?"

I turned and walked down the stairs.

* * *

"Is that chicken ready yet?" the chef shouts at me. I have breadcrumbs and egg all up my arms.

"Almost."

"Service is going to start in 15 minutes."

"Yeah, I know."

"Well, stop fucking around then."

I squeeze the piece of chicken I was crumbing and throw it at the back of the chef's head. It hits his cap and falls onto the ground.

"Does this look like I'm fucking around?" I yell, pointing to the tray piled up with chicken breasts.

The chef turns and stares at me, eyes wide, mouth open. "What the fuck!"

I take off my apron and throw it on the ground.

"Fuck this."

Nicholas comes out the back.

"The customers can hear you," he hisses.

"Fuck the customers!" I yell over his shoulder.

"Just go, man," Nicholas says.

"Don't worry, I am."

I storm out the back, pulling over one of the green bins. It hits the ground, spilling rubbish everywhere. I start walking down the street when my phone begins to ring.

6 ZLATA

WE CANCELLED THE LAST two shows and drove home. The countryside that had been so enchanting on the way down now smirked at us. No one spoke as we drove north. We had escaped the city for a few days and now it was dragging us back. I had never felt so powerless. Right then I knew when I fled I had to leave no word, for fear that place would find me wherever I ran.

We missed the ferry and had to sleep in the car. In the middle of the night I woke with a start. The car was stuffy and I got out for some fresh air. At the water's edge I sat by the shore, watching the waves caress the sand. I tried calling you, but there was no answer.

The next morning we crawled onto the boat and slept on the sticky carpet. We got lunch in Wellington at a Malaysian takeaway joint. No one could eat, so we left our noodles and set out for Auckland. Outside of Foxton it began to rain. It grew heavier and we were forced to slow down.

"I can't see anything," Louisa said quietly, "I just want to get back."

We stopped in Taupo and brought coffee. I managed to reach you. I couldn't tell if you were drunk or crying, probably both. I told you I'd be home round 7 p.m. and that I loved you. I got back into the car and we continued into the storm.

It was dark when we reached the city limits and rain followed us up the motorway. We came over a hill and the lights of the city danced in the distance. The streets were empty; filthy water and trash raced along the gutters. The walls covered in graffiti and peeling posters. We pulled up in front of my house.

"We're home," Louisa said.

5 HAMISH

"IT'S NOT YOUR fault," Zlata keeps saying. We're both crying on our bed. I pick up the bottle of whisky from the floor. Only a mouthful left and I still feel everything. I finish the bottle. Zlata grabs me round the stomach, pulling me into her. We lie like this for hours, crying, reassuring each other, then falling apart again. At some point I pass out. When I wake up, Zlata's already dressed and sitting on the bed.

"You okay?" she asks, her eyes red.

I nod my head even though I can't remember ever feeling worse.

"I just spoke to Rapley and the funeral's in two days."

"I should have gone and seen him," I mutter.

"Don't start that again."

"But I should have."

"Yes, but you didn't and it's too late now."

She comes and sits on the edge of the bed and takes my hand.

"I have to go and do some admin shit for the album," she says. "Stay here and I'll bring us back some lunch."

* * *

Jamil's sitting outside his apartment on a beer crate, wearing a singlet that shows off his fat, pink arms.

"Greetings and salutations," he says.

"Hey."

"Rough month, huh."

"Yeah."

"Well, at least he didn't have to spend 15 years in that fucking place. I was in there for six months and it drove me nuts."

I sit down. "I was going to see if you had any hook-ups for some shit."

"Look at this," he said grinning, "The boot's on the other foot."

"I can't go to my dude; don't want Rapley to find out."

"Yeah, I know someone, but it's not as good as your old shit."

"It'll have to do."

"I thought you were gainfully employed?"

"I was."

"What do you need? I'll call the cunt."

* * *

I get home late and stash the drugs on top of the wardrobe. The house is dark. In the kitchen is a bag of shopping. I check my phone. There's a text from Zlata: "Where are you?"

* * *

I start weighing out the drugs. I'm tense; this wasn't how things were meant to go. But I know Zlata will leave soon. When she was away, I realised how empty this place had become, how I was holding on to my old life, scared. I just have to move some of this shit and we can go anywhere. Things will never be the same here, not after Luke's death. Before that, maybe I could have fixed things. But now it's totally fucked. I stuff the bags into my sock and head out.

4 ZLATA

THINGS HAD ALREADY started when we got to the church. We sat at the back and listened to the priest ramble on about God and forgiveness. Rapley, Sam and everyone were sitting up the front. Behind them was Freckles and half a dozen or so other kids their age. Luke's mother was with a cluster of people on the opposite side of the church, all of them taking turns comforting her. I was cold and leaned into you. You hadn't said more than a couple of words all day. The priest stopped talking and looked out over the small gathering as though waiting for a reply to a question. Some people from the family's side got up and started to carry the coffin outside. Rapley tried to help, but was shooed away. We waited as everyone filed out. All the kids and our friends looking like they were going to court, walking awkwardly in their ill-fitting suits. We got up and followed them outside into the rain. Louisa walked up to us.

"You want to ride with me?" she asked.

At the graveyard, most of the tombstones had fallen over. Some of the graves had been dug up. No one said anything about it. We were standing a short distance from Luke's grave after the burial when a woman around my age walked over, repeatedly straightening her black dress as she approached. She was striking, with long dark hair and pretty blue eyes.

"Hi," she said, "I'm Luke's cousin, Patricia." She stopped and took a deep breath and adjusted herself, "Look, Luke's mother doesn't want you guys at the wake. I'm sorry, but you know …" She looked from one to the other of us nervously.

Louisa stepped forward. "It's fine," she said, hugging her, "I'm so sorry."

Patricia smiled as though a weight had been lifted off her shoulders and walked back to the handful of family.

"Let's go to my place," Louisa said. Everyone began shuffling towards the car park.

"Fuck off!" someone shouted behind us. We turned and saw you and Rapley standing in the middle of the cemetery. Louisa gave me a pained look and we both ran over.

"I'm done with you, man," Rapley said, shoving you, sending you stumbling backwards.

You marched back up to him.

"What?" Rapley shoved you again.

"Rapley," Louisa hissed, pushing him away. "Not here."

I reached out and took your arm. You knocked my hand away.

"Why didn't you fucking go?" Rapley said, his voice cracking. "Why didn't you go?"

Behind him, I could see Luke's family looking over.

"I'm sorry," you said, so quietly that only I heard. You turned and walked away. I ran after you, my shoes sinking into the swampy grass.

"Wait! Don't fucking walk away from me, Hamish," I said, surprised at the desperation in my voice. You didn't even slow. I stopped, watching you disappear as my shoes filled with muddy water.

* * *

I stayed the night on Louisa's couch and woke up to a phone call from work. I mumbled some half-assed excuse and hung up. When I got home you weren't there. Your suit lay in a pile on the floor. I climbed into the cold bed and went back to sleep. It was late in the afternoon when I woke up. I tried your phone but got no answer. I sat on the porch and watched the rain fall on the empty street.

On my way to work the next morning, none of the street lights were on and the dawn was an oily black. I had just sat down at my station when Amber walked past and smiled inanely at me. That's when I knew the game was up. Just before lunch, I was called into the manager's office and told that I was being let go. That's the term they used — so much gentler than fired. She said they would give me two more weeks. I smiled and said I understood, went back to my desk, got my things and left.

Later that afternoon I went up to the label's office. I had to give them the money for the albums I'd sold on tour. The rep greeted me from behind a large cardboard box when I walked in. His greasy black hair was a mess, his shirt was creased.

"Returns from one of the releases," he said, standing up and patting the box.

"Here's the cash; sold 26 in the end." I handed him the fistful of notes.

"It's a shame you had to cancel the last couple of dates." I just stared at him until he started talking again.

"Anyway, the Sydney branch said they're thinking of putting the album out over there." The office stank of raw meat. I looked around, trying to see where it was coming from.

"What do you say? You could tour there."

"Yeah, sure."

* * *

I had a couple of grand in the bank and mum said she'd help out. I was going to pay the ransom and leave that city. Australia wasn't far enough. Half of Auckland lived there. Besides, the album was filled with ghosts. The last thing I wanted was to be haunted by them for another two years. Half my things were still packed from the tour. I got out my suitcase and started stuffing the rest of my clothes into it. I reached on top of the wardrobe to see if my blue beanie was up there and felt something plastic. I knocked it down. A ziplock bag filled with pills and powder hit the floor. I picked it up and stood there holding it for a minute. Then I threw it back up where it came from and kept packing.

"$150 a show is $1200 each," I said, counting out two piles of money.

"We only played six shows," said Louisa, cleaning food off the twin's faces.

"I'm going to pay you for the ones we missed."

"Don't be stupid."

"It's fine." I push the two piles towards them. Sam picked up hers.

"I'm fucking rich." She got up. " I have to go."

"Where you going?" Lou asked, putting the twins down. The two girls ran out of the room, laughing and pushing each other.

"I have a date." Sam started doing a slow 'sexy' dance.

"Who with?"

"No one you know." She put on her leather jacket. "See you losers later."

"Who the fuck is she going on a date with?" Louisa asked.

"Maybe she's tricked Nicholas." We both laughed.

"The label want me to go to Australia, put the album out and tour."

"You want to do it?" A loud crash came from the other room, then a suspicious silence. "Hold on, I'll just make sure they're both still alive."

I picked up Lou's guitar and started playing some chords. My fingers were strong from all the shows. I played a chord progression I had been working on at the soundchecks.

"That sounds nice," Louisa said, coming back into the room. "Is it new?"

I nodded and kept playing.

"So are you going to go?"

I shook my head. "I'm going further."

"Where?"

I kept playing the riff, the four chords making a hypnotic progression.

"I'm not sure yet." I knew exactly where I was going.

"What about Hammy?"

"I don't know. I can't stay here, though."

"I know, if I didn't have the kids …" Louisa looked out the window. "I'll miss you."

"Yeah, I'll miss you too." I stopped playing the guitar. "I really want to know who Sam's date is with."

That night I only checked my phone once.

3 HAMISH

THEY'RE FINALLY LETTING me use the phone.
I call Zlata.

"Hello."

She sounds confused.

"Hey, it's me."

There's a pause. "Hey."

"I'm in the cells."

"What for?"

Now it's my turn to hesitate.

"I got in a fight with a couple of those DMT dudes and had some shit on me when the cops picked me up."

"I found your stash."

"Shhh, not on the phone."

"This isn't *The Wire*. Can I see you?"

"Yeah, they said it's sweet if you come down."

"Okay, I'll see you soon."

I hang up. A cop walks me back to the cell. I've got no belt or laces so I have to shuffle like a dickhead. Back in the cell I scratch my tag into the wall for the hundredth time.

* * *

I'm lying on the bench, hoodie over my eyes, when the cop comes back in.

"Get up, asshole, your missus is here." He leads me to a small room, empty except for a table and a couple of chairs. It's so comfortable after sleeping on that shitty bed. The door opens; Zlata walks in. She smiles quickly. We hug and then she sits down and stares at me. Her beautiful eyes are red.

"How long have you been selling again?" she asks without any emotion.

"Just a few days, I wanted to get some money for us." I whisper.

She nods.

"So what happens now?"

"Sentencing is in a couple of days. I don't think I'll do much time. Maybe six months."

"Oh god." She sinks further into her chair.

"It's okay, baby. I'll be out and then we can go somewhere."

She stares at me for a long time. I can tell she's trying not to cry. Then she smiles.

"Of course."

"It'll be fine, just a few months."

"Of course."

"I love you, Zlata."

She gets up and kisses me. "I'll see you in court," she says, then walks out.

* * *

Back in the cell, I kill time looking at the tags, seeing who's been in here before me. Jamil and Skam are both up everywhere; judging by the different pens, they've been in a few times. Thank fucking god I haven't spent the last two nights in a cell with Jamil. I'm taking a piss when I see Luke's tag in the cubicle. He'd never been locked up before the stabbing. This must have been where they sent him. My legs feel weak. I go and sit down.

When you're locked up, you don't really have a present, so you're forced to think about the past or the future. The past was one fucking disaster after another, so instead I imagine a future with Zlata. I think about us overseas. Japan is the only place I've been, so everywhere looks like Tokyo. I think about us exploring together; Zlata talking fast, how she does. I think about her love, her lips and body, those eyes, the way they looked when we first got together, before all this bullshit piled up on top of us. I think about how, despite everything, she still loves me, and I realise things will be okay. I just have to get out of here as soon as I can. I relax and try to sleep.

2 ZLATA

IN THE DAYS leading up to your court case the streets were filled with whispers. Everyone watched from behind streaked windowpanes and manic grins. I spent hours on the deck drinking, picking off bits of rotten wood and throwing them onto the footpath. I silently cursed you, the cowardice you masked with stony bravado, the anger cradled in your tattooed arms, the fierce naïvety you wore like a medal.

At night, the whispering became laughter. It danced down the rubble that was once our road, deafening. I lay in bed, listening to it grow closer. It would stop outside the house, a howling storm of gossip and ridicule. I pulled the duvet over my head and waited for morning to restore a fragile reality. The days were hung over and sleep-deprived. I said yes to everything — the tour of Australia, Hayley's dinner party, the job Jess had found me — and tiptoed from the house to the bottle store and back again, waiting.

I called my mother and told her what was happening.

She comforted me without lying. Said that things would be difficult, but that I would be okay. I listened and cried quietly until I ran out of credit.

The day before sentencing, Louisa came over. We caught the bus out to Luke's grave. The dirt was still fresh. We stood there holding hands, not knowing what to say. It was impossible to equate this pile of dirt and piece of stone with Luke.

"I keep expecting him to turn up at my house," Louisa said, "with some stolen bottle of booze."

I laughed.

"I think I even miss his stupid songs," I said.

Louisa started to cry. "Shit," she wiped her eyes with her sleeve. "What a fucking year."

* * *

Afterwards we sat on the deck drinking some shitty red wine.

"Tomorrow's the day," she said.

"I hate this."

"I know." She grabbed my hand and then smiled. "So, Sam was on a date with some handsome guy."

"Really?"

"Yeah, he's like two feet taller than her."

"Wow."

A group of children ran by with a pack of dogs. They stopped outside the gate, their faces covered in war paint. They pointed and laughed and the dogs howled and barked and then they ran on.

"I think he's rich too," Louisa said, passing me back the bottle.

* * *

On the day of the court case I got up early. In the bathroom I brushed my hair and stared at the determined-looking woman watching me. We stood like that for a long time. She didn't take her burning blue eyes off me once. Then, without warning, she smiled and I found myself smiling back. I took a deep breath and called a cab.

1 HAMISH

THE PADDY WAGON'S FULL. No one talks. We drive the short distance to the courthouse, then we're led into another cell. One of the cops takes off our handcuffs and everyone sits down, rubbing their wrists. I try to get comfortable but my back is killing me. A couple of guys in the corner are talking shit, both trying to show off with bullshit stories about crime and violence.

The holding room's got the same beige walls and ugly carpet as every other government institution I've been in. Could just as easy be in the hospital waiting room on a Saturday night filled with booze and broken glass, or in WINZ about to beg for enough money to eat.

After a couple of hours I get taken to see the legal aid lawyer. In a tiny office I sit opposite a woman in a cheap suit. She blows her nose loudly.

"Sorry," she says. "So, you're in here for assault and drug possession?"

"Yeah."

"How do you want to plead?"

"Guilty for the drugs; the fight was self-defence."

"There's a witness statement here that says you walked onto a crowded dance floor and started punching the victim."

"Yeah, nah, it wasn't like that."

"What was it like then?" She blows her nose again and stuffs the handkerchief in her sleeve.

"I was trying to help my friend and I was attacked."

"Okay, well, I guess we'll see what the judge thinks."

I'm led back into the cells to wait for another couple of hours.

I think about getting out of here. I'm excited to travel. I won't be able to go to the States if I get the drug conviction, but Zlata always talked of more exciting places. Wish we'd gone earlier, but there's no point thinking that way. The last time I was in this position I was scared, but not now. Today I'm calm. It's different knowing she's waiting for me. If I can get off the assault charge I'll probably only be away a month or two. Can use that time to make more art and sell that shit when I get out. It'd be easy. Rapley was right — why not take those rich people's money? I hated how weak I was sometimes. I should have talked to Zlata. But it's hard — no one wants to hear about your problems. I guess they find out anyway.

* * *

The cop comes in and leads me out to the courtroom. I walk into the dock. It's bright and filled with people. The sudden change shocks me. I rub my eyes, look out over the crowd. The lawyer's still blowing her nose; behind her are Sam and Louisa. They smile and wave at me. I can't see

Zlata anywhere. My lawyer gets up and starts talking but I can't hear her over the ringing in my ears. One of the cops that arrested me stands up, starts reading out all my past convictions. Again I scan the crowd but still can't see her. My stomach tightens. The lawyer's talking again.

"The defendant is claiming self-defence on the assault charge."

The cop smirks at me. Smug motherfucker. The prosecution lawyer reads out the witness statement and I wonder who made it. The judge asks me if I have anything to say. I shake my head.

"Six month suspended sentence," he says, "with a curfew."

I'm taken back out to the cell, my legs barely supporting me.

When I'm released, Louisa and Sam are waiting outside the court. A light rain is falling.

We hug and walk towards where they're parked.

"Where's Zlata?" I ask, as we're driving back to Grey Lynn. I've been waiting for them to tell me, but they both sit silently in the front, staring out the windscreen as the wipers push the rain aside.

"She's gone," Louisa says quietly.

"Where?" My voice high-pitched.

"I don't know, babe. We went to get her this morning and all her stuff's gone."

Sam reaches back and grabs my hand. We drive in silence for a bit. It's only 5 p.m. but it's already getting dark.

"At least you're free," Louisa says, as we head down Williamson Ave.

EPILOGUE

IT'S MIDNIGHT BUT it looks like dawn. You could point a camera in any direction and capture a photo worthy of a postcard. Everything is green except a few houses, tumours on a naked landscape. It would be easy to go mad here, to let go of that thin thread, and be consumed. Some nights I feel my fingers loosen and I smile. I know I'm safe, shielded from the elements by years spent in a wasteland.

The summers are timeless, a single day stretching for three months. I often find myself climbing the cliffs behind my house at 2 a.m., the sun still high above me. I stand at the edge, watching parts of the earth fall into the ocean, consumed by the waves. The path cuts into the side of the cliff: one wrong step and I would join the bits of rock and earth among the ocean. They don't bother with illusions of safety here and there's something comforting in that.

Birds nest along the paths. You have to watch your step so as not to tread on a pile of eggs or kick a hatchling into the abyss. Often the parents become agitated, swooping and squawking at me. But it doesn't hurt when they peck my head so I no longer fight them off. People say there are seals that come up on the beaches below the cliffs but I've yet to see them. Some nights I sit with my feet dangling over the edge, watching the beach, wondering if every rock is actually a seal.

I work full-time on a farm. The job is hard but the people are friendly. I have no car and have to walk for an hour every morning along empty roads. My pay covers rent and food. There is nothing else to spend money on here anyway. The rest of the time I write songs and cook. I wish you could see my cooking now; necessity has made me competent in the kitchen. I no longer live on baked beans and toast. There is only one place to eat out here, where the food drips yellow grease onto off-white plates. On weekends, the village gathers here to drink and forget among the artificial dusk. Nothing is as blinding as the midnight sun after a few vodkas.

My songwriting has improved as well. They are simpler now, stripped back to the bones. There are no shows or labels any more, I'm writing only for myself. I think of you whenever I sit down and compose. My mother was right; you are my muse.

The only person who hears my songs is the art teacher, Maria. We have bonded over a shared love of dancing and vodka. She is from the capital so is also considered an outsider. Maria is short and beautiful, her eyes an intense blue that matches the Icelandic sky. Some weekends she will turn up with a bottle and we'll drink and fly around the room in time to whatever music we can find. Afterwards, we'll lie together on the couch, our faces flushed, and I'll play her my songs. She says you sound like a bad man. I no longer defend you.

* * *

I've been here three times as long as we were together and not a day goes by when I don't think of you, or a night where you don't invade my dreams. Some mornings my mind is clear for a few seconds and then you enter and refuse to leave all day. There's a masochistic comfort in having you close.

They have the internet here but I refuse to use it. I don't want to know what's happening. I picture the worst. But then remember you proved to me that my imagination isn't capable of that. What difference does it make anyway? That city could be levelled and everyone I know dead; it would change nothing. I don't even have a cell phone. Even if I could talk to you, my family and friends, what else is there to say?

My days have been reduced to a simple routine. I wake at 6 a.m. on weekdays, drink a coffee and set off for the farm. After work I walk home, make dinner and then read or write till I fall asleep. This description does nothing to explain what the days are like.

Some nights I drink alone and fall around the apartment, knocking over chairs, alternating between crying and laughing, and wake up covered in bruises. It reminds me of you.

Maria talks about moving somewhere smaller. Her best friend lives on an island of 50 people off the coast. She says it'll be better. I don't know if this is an invitation. I sometimes wonder if I would go. What would I do? But then there is little here for me either. Sometimes I sit and stare at the mountain and realise for the first time in my life I am completely free. It is hard to put into words how much this terrifies me.

* * *

Your letter sliced a hole in the belly of my new life. The blood and shit of the past poured out over the floor. I found myself thinking of life back on the other side of the world. I assume you got my address from my mother; she is the only person who knows that I'm here. It sat on the kitchen table, screaming at me while I made coffee.

The sky was a dark blue as I made my way along the side of the dirt road. Work was slow. I sang as I collected eggs from the chickens. I missed the only sunlight, cleaning the cowshed. Maria picked me up. I love how she knows what I need even when I don't. We took a bath together. I ran my hands over the curves of her beautiful compact body. Afterwards, we sat outside and shared a joint. The Northern Lights dance above us.

"I'm going to move to the island soon," she said, exhaling. "You should come."

I sat there, watching the lights, without speaking for a long time. Then, walking inside, I got your letter. I came back out, took Maria's lighter and set fire to one end of the envelope. I held it till the flames almost reached my fingers then dropped it and watched it burn in the snow.

What else is there to say.

ACKNOWLEDGEMENTS

Special thanks to Jeff and May, without you guys none of this would have happened.

Thanks to everyone who took the time to read all the early drafts of this book and help turn it into something readable.

Love and kisses to all of you who supported my crowd-funding campaign to go to Iceland and write this thing:

Gus Simonovic, Laura Vincent, Andrew Henry, Kerry Ann Lee, Steve Boyd, Adam Branson, Adrian Farrugia, Hayden Pyke, Sean Bonniface, Sarah-Jean Thomas, Laura Deverell, Martyn Pepperell, Jeremy Raine, Georgia Schofield, Hamish Pattison, Kathryn Higgins, Charlotte Collier-Hunter, Thomas Scovell, Matt Rapley, Dylan Chase, Will Wood, Louise Petch, Zlata Kozhemyako, Harley Wooller, Louisa Jones, Glenn Elliott, Haylee Mitchell, Hamish Clulee, Nicholas FitzHerbert, Jamil Geor, Kate Rylatt, Mark Rickerby, Alice Andersen, Bella DuBois, Beatrix Coles, Jono Kerr, Samuel Walsh, Dawn Peters, Ben Thomas, Ashleigh Cox, Sean Bonniface, Victoria King, Jules Longdin-Prisk, Colin Mitchell, Lucha Lounge (RIP Karyn), Mieke van der Walle, and Joni Roper-Hughes.

As part of the crowdfunding campaign, backers could have characters named after them. Characters in this novel resemble these people in name only.

ABOUT THE AUTHOR

DOMINIC HOEY is a poet, author and musician based in Auckland, New Zealand. Under the Tourettes moniker he has released five critically acclaimed studio albums, two books of poetry and four short films. In a former life, he was an MC battle and slam-poetry champion, and has performed his spoken-word poetry in Australia, Europe, England, Japan and America. Dominic also works as an arts mentor, teaching rangatahi excluded from mainstream education.